The Nations: Fraternity

A. Ruben

Printed in the United States of America.

The Nations: Fraternity / Ruben

ISBN: 978-0-9754590-8-9

Ickynicks Publishing

Front Cover by Adam Zillins

Illustrations by Adam Talley

Artwork (Maps) by A. Ruben

The following story is entirely fictional. Any similarity to any actual event or person is entirely coincidental and unintentional.

The Globe

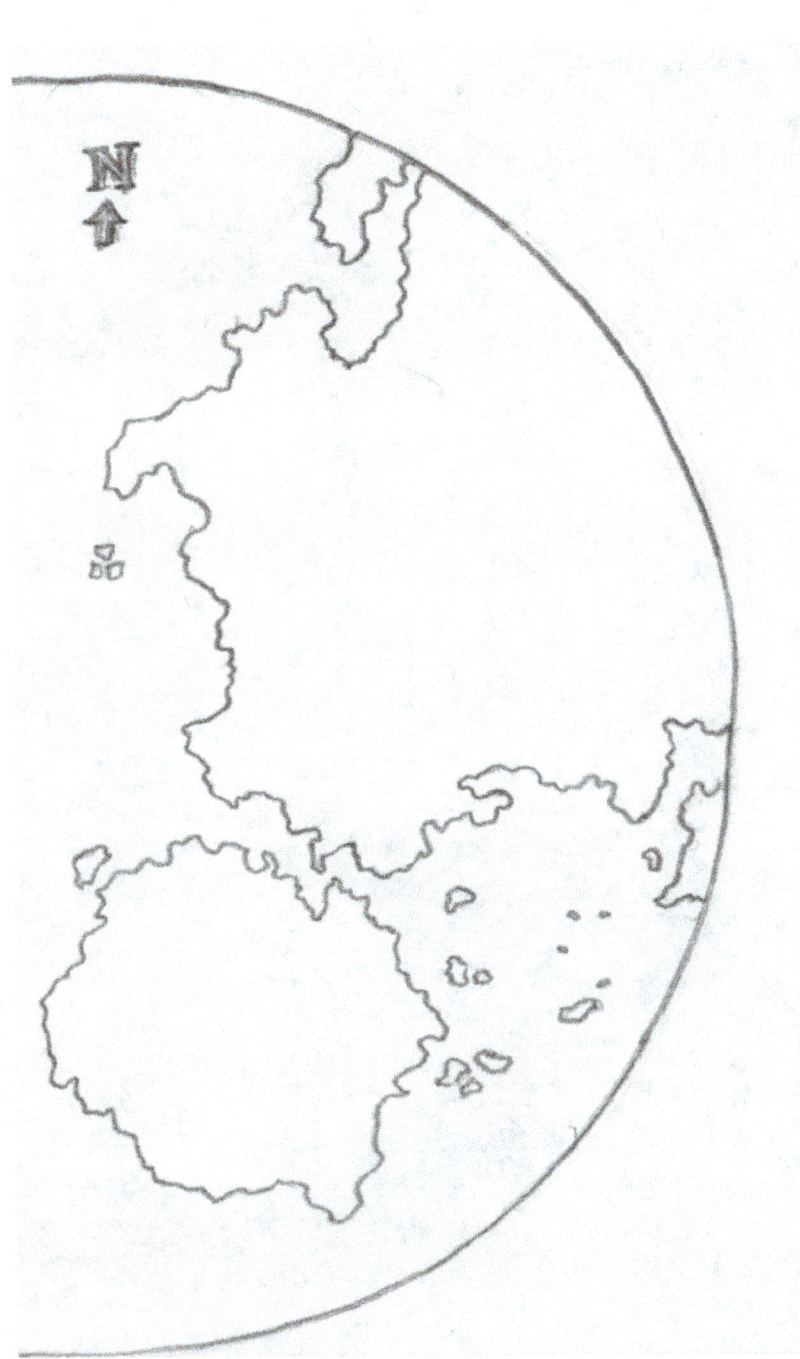

The "New World"

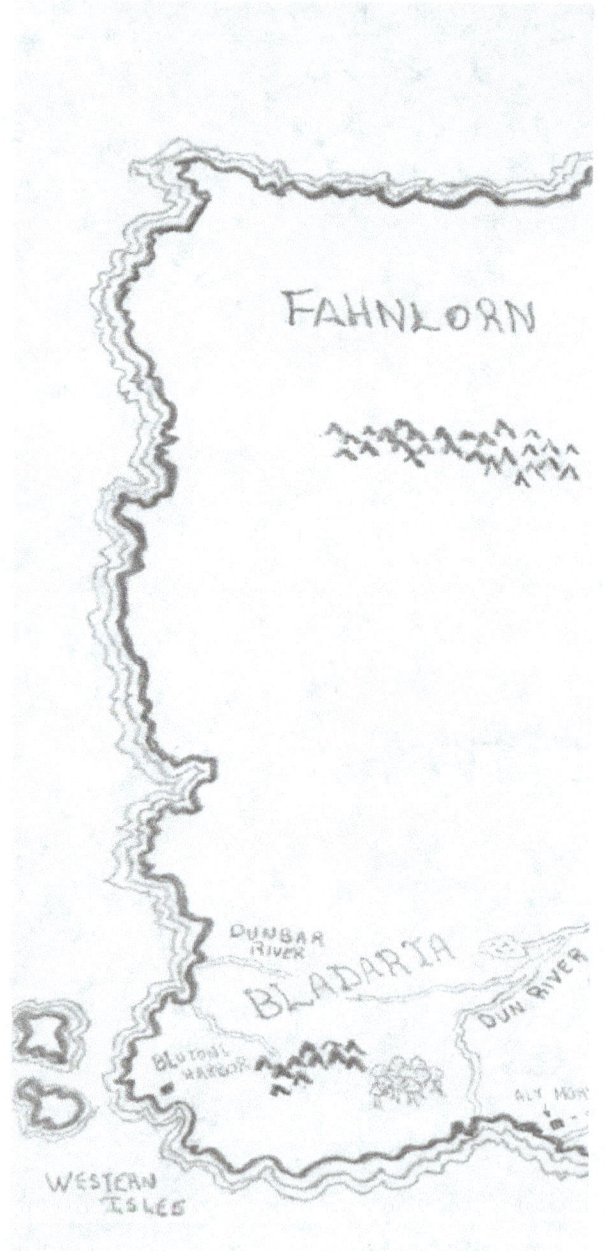

The Major Power of Romennal

Strait of Romennal

St. Pierra Thongs

Martas

In memory of Ed & Pauline. For the stories they shared with their grandson.

Acknowledgements

The author wishes to thank the following for their support, Lynn, Marilyn, Adam, Neil, Mark, Alex, Sara, Rochelle and Mike. Thank you very much for your assistance in making this work possible.

Chapters

Chapter 1

The Shot Heard Around the World

Leopaln stepped one foot at a time down the plank, inching closer with each step not realizing how much he had missed land. The past three months at sea had been quite unpleasant; heaving over the side each day was as unbearable as the confining of his tight quarters where the swaying of the ocean waves rocked him to and fro each night such that he hardly slept a moment.

In fact, as he conceded to himself, he felt unquestionably miserable of it all. As the waves were like a perpetual rhythm of torment upon his poor stomach, emaciating his soul with a malady of dislike for the accursed thing that he now detested the wretchedness of seasickness much more so than ever before.

And yet, as the days passed with no end to his eternal torment he cursed the expansive vastness before him and prayed daily for the call of land; anything else was preferred, even the coming of Judgment Day. Hallelujah. But as the sea was unforgiving so was his regret for ever coming aboard; though he kept a vigil watch to the sea, hoping for some sign like a floating branch or a seagull, he knew it had been a terrible mistake to embark into the matriarch of emptiness. He cursed the waters and pondered how others could breath in its salty repugnance; a sailor's life was not his. He was a soldier. He belonged to the land and it to him; he craved to hear the sounding call of land, and knew with each day he must be getting closer.

But alas, as the sands of time trickle away ever so slowly so too were the calls of the quartermaster's mate half-hour calls, taunting him, teasing him, and toying with his longing desire to set foot upon land once more. He missed it as much as he missed his love; how they played around the garden as children and kissed for the first time by the creek that warm summer afternoon.

She was so beautiful. Her flowing hair glistened in the sunlight as he rolled it behind her ear; her melodic voice appealed to the youngling birds nestling above them in the great oak on his family's estate.

He smiled pleasantly to the memory. "I will be home soon," he had promised her, sorely wishing he could turn the ship around now. He had never wanted to leave her, but it was his duty after all. He was an officer, and though his father had tried to persuade him to stay his youthful fervor would not keep to the comforts of a desk. He longed for adventure and to see the world.

"You are foolhardy," his father had said, irate at his impudent decision to waste away an inheritance. It was their last discourse before he had stormed out.

"I am old enough, father."

"You are a child!"

"I am nearly nineteen," he said, which was a comment dismissed as quickly as it was said.

"You are a boy, and have no idea of the world around you. I have tried to enlighten you, but clearly you have failed to absorb my lessons!"

"I am an officer, father," as if that was persuasive.

"At my discretion," he snapped at his insolence. "How dare you presume to think that you earned that title on your own disposition! You are of my house, and of my lineage, and you will pay that respect! You are a teenager with no conception of the world outside my walls," he added, berating him, and treating him like a child. "You live and breath at my good graces and your fantasy with Ms. Evelyn will end when I say it will. You will marry of proper gentry as it should be!"

"I'm sorry father, but no."

"What did you say," he said, exploding. "HOW DARE YOU DEFY ME IN MY OWN HOME! Are you so daft a child as to rebel against me as those colonials of our great nation? You are an impudent disgrace to this family's name. You are a child in the ways of this world, filled with ideals and stories that should have been put to bed years ago; as should this affair with Ms. Evelyn."

"I love her, father!"

"Oh quiet boy," he said, almost laughing at that absurdity. "Your romantic interest in her is nothing but cosmetics to satisfy your boyish desires. How could you possibly marry such a trifle as her? And God forbid you so shamelessly rush off and leave her with only a name to carry and a child in her womb. You would have undone this family's good name and burglarized us of this estate's fortune."

"She's not a thief, father."

"Oh wake up boy. She's a pauper charming your heart to reach into your pockets; your mother is in the other room beside herself with grief that you would so recklessly deprive her of a rightful heir! You should be ashamed of yourself."

Leopaln had no reply then but to turn his back, but now as the waves crashed against the hull he had plenty of time to consider how he would have replied. Perhaps he had been selfish, but she had understood. She had embraced him with all the love in her heart, and in exchange he gave her his love under that same oak tree. She knew he would return.

4

The Nations: Fraternity

And everyday since then, he thought of her, waiting for the moment to feel her warmth again. She was his world. She gave him strength when he poured his stomach over the side and collapsed in his cabin, exhausted and weak; he pulled out her yellow handkerchief from his pocket and held it to his heart. She meant everything to him.

And though he was ill from the sea he did all he could to render his spirits high, making the best of his time so as to distract himself from the cruel measure of the sea. He sedated himself by wandering aimlessly about the ship, conversing with others and appeasing his curiosity as to how things worked. He enjoyed learning; at night, he joined with the other officers at dinner, sharing wine and stories.

"To hell with the colonies," a veteran said one evening. He had had far too much to drink. "It is purgatory, a land where stairs only lead downwards and a place only fit for wives."

The married laughed and toasted to his swagger while the bachelors raised their glasses if only to keep the merriment going and the wine coming. Leopaln did neither, but took offense instead. "We have our orders, and we will do our duty, so speak ill of it all you want but that is where we're headed, and that's where our brethren be."

"Perhaps," the senior officer replied, indignant at his youthful naivety and vinegar. "But my boy, ale and wine make fine leisure fellows, so please leave the austere at the door. We are but the rancid of society and to waste spirits or wine is as criminal as the wretched worms we sail to," he said in a drunken stupor. "So my advice to you is to drink up and be less yourself tonight. Perhaps we may yet make a man of you," he said to a resounding ovation.

"And we wonder why they declared independence," Leopaln muttered to himself, taking a sip. He was repulsed by the man's drunkenness as well as his apparent aversion to proper decorum; sobriety made a gentleman refined, but self-control tempered his balance between depravity and etiquette.

He was an officer like them, but they had years ahead of him and saw the world from cynical eyes. His father had tried to teach him, but only experience would now be his mentor. "Be open, Leopaln," his father had said to him as a boy. He had held him in his arms as he showed him his library; the young boy beheld shelves of books and maps, but gazed in wonder at the large globe in the center of the room.

"The world is as big as you want it to be, or as small. But beware, the more you open your mind the fewer there will be who share your opinion." He set the boy down and allowed him to explore the globe, touching its surface and spinning it in wonderment. "One day, you may yet see it for yourself."

The Nations: Fraternity

But that was a long time ago, and just as he was amazed at the oceans on the globe so now he was crossing one; he respected his father, but despite being so far from him he still felt animosity. The man could instruct others, but failed to guide him; he demanded when he perhaps should have compromised. But that wasn't the man's way. He was cold and calculated, never resigning or wavering in his opinion, even for his own son.

And as the rain poured heavily on the deck and Leopaln was confined to his cabin, he was sure this torrential weather was in some measure his fault for dishonoring his father. Surely, there was a whale out there to consume him for his sins; and all night the storm lasted, loosening his stomach onto the floor and rendering him sleepless.

As he finally drifted off a slight tap came at his door. "Hope you rested well," came the accented voice of the midshipman, failing to hide his chuckle. "Up and out with ye. The morning air awaits."

"Be gone and let me sleep," he shouted in a groggy and hardly discernable voice, but the tapping came again, as the man knew he had no love for the sea and enjoyed teasing him. "Curse you to the bottom of this monstrosity. For all that is holy, let me sleep!" But when the tapping became louder he resigned to defeat and dragged himself into the light. "When the world comes to an end I shall personally see to it that you are the last to enter the gates of paradise," but the man just smiled and began singing, reveling to the pain that his voice caused.

"'Tis these decks that makes a man, and a sea that calls to me! Glory Be!"

"Curse you're rattling. Please, I wish to hear no more. Truly, you are the devil reincarnate."

"You're too kind," he laughed, then gazing out to sea and pointed to the horizon. "Look there," he said. "I may be the devil, but that is a sight to behold. Surely, it is the signature of the Lord, if he could write!"

"Indeed," Leopaln agreed, slowly awakening. It was as brilliant and beautiful as his love back home. The morning air was filling his lungs, and as much as he wanted to return to his cabin he was now too alert to give up the day. "Well, how say you of land?" he asked, hopeful. "Is it favorable or has misfortune yet again bestowed upon us another day of this confounded misery?"

"Nay sir, same waters as yesterday and the day before and the day yonder that," the man replied, breathing in the salty ocean air. "Aye, land rings fine in your ears, but not mine. Truth is my preference is here; too many years at sea and you begin to accept this vastness as your own." He grinned happily. "Aye, here I'm home."

"Yes, home is nice."

"That it be, but never you fear, sire, we shall land for you soon, if Heaven protects us of course; too many evils about," he said, as if still harboring archaic fears of mythical monsters of the sea. He peered over the edge frightfully, amusing the officer with his obsolete superstition.

"The only thing Heaven is protecting us against," Leopaln said, "is your wild imagination."

"Pray that is true," the man smiled, "because now I've gone and frightened myself," he said, laughing too. The two went and got something to eat.

"So what have you heard about the colonies?" Leopaln asked as they partook of breakfast; he had avoided speaking of it, but as each day brought him closer he knew he ought to ask.

"Rumors only," the sailor said. "From what I hear, there's no place worse. They're savage beasts."

"How so?"

"They shoot officers first," he said, making Leopaln shift uncomfortably. That was unsettling. "Aye, barbarians are what they are; illegitimate bastards of our great nation, born too far away to be grateful for what they've been given, and too distant to even want it. So, instead they throw their fists in the air and curse our beloved king, their king.

"It's a forsaken land. Aye, they may be of similar blood, but certainly they're not of the same mind; I'm no soldier, just an old sailor who talks nonsense and looks to the waters for monsters," he half-joked, gazing out to sea. "Aye, she's a beauty. Lethal but majestic."

Leopaln shared his sentiment. The sun was breaching the horizon and illuminating the sky. "I'm a religious man, sir. Nothing but that holds my two feet to the ground. I like to think of myself as being sensible to Heaven, but who knows these things. I just do my part, for Man and God; but those folk over there in the colonies do neither. They respect neither their king nor God; to disregard the sovereignty of one is to deny the other. Respect, sir, that's what matters in this life. It's all a man has in this world. He may need to fight his fellow man, but he does so with respect; and shooting officers is anything but that."

The colonials had achieved initial successes, storming an arsenal and surprising a reserve that was sent to recapture it. "Hardly worth celebrating," the midshipman said. "War is like religion, sir. It must have rules that demand our strict adherence, lest we tear ourselves asunder. That is the reason why gentlemen must lead, because they are the last bastion of chivalry in this world; to exchange courtesy and sensibility on the field is what sets us apart from the animals that tear at each other; to allow our enemy the right of first volley is an honor to those that die and the greatest show of respect that one man can give to another."

With their initial triumphs, scores of rebel colonists had begun trespassing onto loyalist plantations, confiscating wares of silver and gold and stealing livestock; businesses too have come under attack, some being burned after being ransacked; what one side claimed to be illegal the other side declared as a right from God.

Having inhabited this so-called "New World" a century earlier to escape persecution they had begun life anew, building homes and interacting with the natives to cultivate plants. But a century of hardship and a vast ocean in between had corrupted their sense of virtue, discipline, and respect towards the throne that had allowed safe exodus in the first place; whatever qualities they had possessed had since been supplanted or forsaken.

"Nothing but a festering cesspool," the midshipman added, remarking how a once fledging dream had reverted into a society of barbarism and usurpation, demanding rights like a child tantrums over a toy. "He that once paid tribute with laurels to the crown now spits upon it."

They had severed all ties of ancestry, blood, and kinship, and had taken up arms like misguided children, not only challenging their parent but daring his corrective hand of justice; His Majesty was no stranger to war and was as resolute in his conviction to rehabilitate their anarchical philosophies that now ran amok as he was in quelling the radical pamphleteers who printed libel and denounced the crown with preposterous notions of what they called the inherent rights of mankind.

"Man must be ruled," the sailor said, sharing his opinion openly. "Otherwise he is but an animal, taking what he wants when he wants; laws are what tame us. We are born as beasts from the womb, and a good parent teaches us temperance; if not, then man will murder, rape and steal. It is an absolute will that governs and cradles us into a harmony of prosperity; civilization depends upon it. Only then can man advance himself from the beast he is; he must be willing to sacrifice his own desires for the greater good, and if he is unwilling then he must be forced."

As Leopaln listened he felt moved by his words, and more reassured of his purpose. "Where will be dock then?" he asked. The man shuttered at the thought. "Clarkstown," he said. "The largest port in the colonies, and the womb of rebellion."

Clarkstown was indeed the largest port-city in the colonies as well as its worst offender of insolence, for in its erroneous ideology it had committed the ultimate act of transgression by decimating goods into the harbor water; all over, streets overflowed with misguidance and boldness, shouting and cursing as well as taunts and dares that prompted swift remedial action by the garrison, including martial law and the institution of a strict curfew; what one side declared as the preservation of law and order the lateral denounced as oppression.

But neither the Crown nor Parliament was satisfied and demanded restitution as well a quarantine of all imports and exports, arresting trade to serve as a lesson against such insurrection and malicious acts of depravity; moreover, a bill was swiftly passed providing for the search and seizure of all colonial vessels and homes in order to root out the lawless; the newspapers on both sides reported on the subsequent riots that followed and the martyrs that fell.

And as jails filled so did the headlines. News of the civil uprisings in Clarkstown rippled across the colonies; it was the caviar of gossip, and newspapers sold out. A savoring flavor to the palate, the unfolding events captured the imagination of even the most illiterate abroad. From Clarkstown, the flames of revolution spread and all but the newspapers worried; as profits soared, only the opportunist hoped for more.

As the numbers continued to escalate in property damage and fatalities, forever immortalizing the fallen, the public demanded action; when sentries defending their post were assailed by a mob and shots were fired the public demanded justice; but whereas colonials wanted hangings the loyalist public insisted on condemnation of the heretical radicals. And to add to the boiling pot, the colonial newspapers printed the story as a massacre instead of what it was, an unarmed mob daring soldiers to fire upon them; it was as unjust in its imagery as it was in its slant, stirring sentiment towards riotous action and defaming the king as a savage despot.

But His Majesty was anything but that. From a long lineage, both proud and benevolent, his family had served admirably, except for a few unscrupulous names, and given the nation a standing among nations; it was a power to be reckoned with. Her fleet was unparalleled and her armies disciplined; valiant in the field as she was at sea, the nation and its people took pride in their nationalism and fealty to the crown. Unto their children, they passed these legacies and generation after generation each served with distinction.

And in difficult times and in good times, the Crown had persevered, compromising authority with a Parliament body, and before the House of Lords, His Majesty proclaimed that with their blessing he would right the wrongs of the colonies and restore order with all the power entrusted to him and cheers resounded.

The Nations: Fraternity

And like so many others, Leopaln was headed across the sea, awaiting a fate he knew not. All he did know was that this was only the beginning, and as the midshipman said, chuckling to himself as if foretelling what was certainly forthcoming, "At least when the waves hit your hull you know you aren't going down with the ship; best be thrown to one side of the ship than be stuck with a ball in your belly."

Chapter 2

Arriving at Clarkstown

Purgatory. It was the name some gave to the colonies, where a once promising dream had died. As Leopaln stared out to sea he remembered his father telling him about it as a child. It was a place built on dreams, but that was the problem. What happens when two dreams collide? "How can you build a house where one already exists," he had asked his father so long ago.

"That is the challenge," he had replied, pointing to the large globe in his study. "The world is built upon dreams, needs, and wants. But the same dream cannot be shared in the same space as another. So sometimes one dream has to be pushed aside for another, a better one."

"So we replaced their homes?" he asked, bemused.

His father nodded. "Man must build his house to last. We build our homes out of brick. We move on wheels and horses and sail. The natives know nothing of this, and so we must educate them, show them our ways and help bring them into our customs and ways of life."

"But don't they have a way of life already?"

"They do," his father said affectionately, "but it is the obligation of a superior man to guide his fellow man, much like an older brother takes the hand of a younger. We must do all that we can to improve their way of life, and even if they resist it is our duty to give them civility." He paused. "Now spin it," he said.

Leopaln happily spun the world. It circled wildly on its axis. "It goes around and around," he giggled.

"It is round," his father said. "But at one time, man wasn't sure about that, and feared falling off; he thought the world was flat, but it took a dream to prove that wrong. So do you see? One dream must replace another. Now we know the world is round. Now we are more intelligent and determined than those before us. That is how it is. The world is always replaced by the dreams of others, and that you must remember."

The ocean spray hit his face and he returned to the present. He remembered happy moments, but didn't forget the animosity in his heart. As he wiped his face his thoughts lingered back to his father's globe. It had always interested him. He remembered marveling at it; to his childish eyes, it filled the room.

His father had showed him where places were, including the colonies, but the so-called New World was hardly uninhabited. Populated by natives, it was also home to several fledging nations that while inferior to His Majesty's armada and armies were formidable in their own right; they had sovereigns of their own and possessed rich histories of war and peace, expansion and trade, and enough politics to rival any.

These advanced nations inhabited the north and south of the New World, but left the central region to the natives, as only their histories could answer why; they warred with another, but such was their history that none dared to colonize or annex land in the center out of trepidation of the past being repeated. Such was the history, Leopaln was told about as a child. "Who lives there," he once asked his father, his mind returning to the past. His finger pointed a spot on the globe that read *Unclaimed Territory*.

"The natives do," he answered.

"But what does unclaimed mean?"

"It means not taken by anyone."

"But I thought you said people already lived there?"

"Indeed they do, but remember what I said. An older brother must care for his younger and these people have no king or laws or sense of civilization as advanced as ours and so they must be looked after. They hunt and gather for their food and although they do farm they lack the irrigation systems like we have. They are wild."

"Like animals?"

"Do not mistake men for animals, Leopaln," his father corrected him sternly. "It may seem that way, but these people have homes, just as you and I do. The difference is how far one strives to improve and with what resources can one maximize to that end. These natives may wish to advance themselves, but they cannot do so quickly without our help, and so that is why it rests upon our shoulders to one day claim that land and do all that we can to assist them."

"But why hasn't anyone else done that yet?" The globe showed six other advanced nations on the same continent as the natives.

"Because of a treaty made long ago."

"What's a treaty?"

"It's like a promise."

"What did they promise?"

"I will tell you one day," he said, smiling at his inquisitive manner. "But I will share with you that something terrible happened that made them all come together and make a promise, and none of them have yet broken that."

19

"When did they make that promise?"

"More than a hundred years ago."

"That's a long time I guess."

"It is, and remember this Leopaln, promises are important. So important in fact that when you make a promise with someone it is your word, and in this world a man's word it is all he has. Your word is your bond, so never break it."

"I promise," he said with a smile.

The sun was high in the sky now, and the ship pushed against the waves; the sails were full of wind and making good time. Soon it would arrive at Clarkstown, and Leopaln would set foot in a place he had only ever seen on a globe; he had been at the academy when word came about the rebellion and many of his friends had been shipped over. But his father had pulled some strings and had him arranged for a desk job.

"You told me to never break a promise and I have a duty to go!" he shouted at him, but his father only dismissed his boyish sentiment. "You'll thank me in years to come," he said, unwaveringly.

Since the day he had stormed out, he hadn't looked back. Perhaps spoiled, perhaps ungrateful, but he nevertheless refused to be told what to do any longer; he was a man and would determine his own fate far from a domineering parent.

He had a duty to fulfill and if that meant being disrespectful for an instant then so be it; every man has a right to stand on his own two feet, his father had once said, and now he had done just that. All that he had to do now was persevere and never falter.

The thought of the colonies troubled him, and strangely excited him. He was braving a new world, taking a first step into the unknown and pushing himself to become something more than what he was; he was unsure of what it would be like, but somehow he felt confident that whatever he experienced he could handle; in his heart, he knew he was ready for this.

And though he felt fear, his courage prevailed and commandeered his anxiety, brushing it aside; he could do this. He was an officer and well trained. And though he missed home and his love, he knew he would see them again. And as he pulled out his book, he reminded himself of the promises he had made and meant to keep. *I will see you again, my love,"* he vowed. Opening it up, he read a passage that offered some comfort. It was a book he had borrowed from his father's library, and it told the history of where he was going, of the advanced nations and the natives, and the great treaty that was signed:

T'was a plague they said, all death around, and nothing but the ashes of lost souls to comfort the bereaved. A gaze beyond the ruins saw the rising smoke off the fields and the flies in a buzzard above the cattle carcasses in the pastures. Fences were battered with lifeless bodies scattered about. The defending had fallen, but not to raiders or a pestering neighbor. No, t'was was an army led by He who is called Goshen. He, who was found on top of a hill echoing the cry to war and gathered men to His call, and these men, the Men of the Land of Bladaria followed Him and marched forth with Him. And all who marched with Him fought for Him and died for Him. Wandering into these ruins, a place once called home, the whisper of His name   was   all   that   remained.

And as his voyage neared its end, Leopaln awaited the anticipated and inescapable sounding of land. How close that day was! With shouts of glee and cheers, the months at sea would at last be over; every morning he hoped, and just as he despaired a sailor sighted port in the thicket of the morning fog. "Gulls, gulls, I hear seagulls!" He shouted excitedly. At once, the ship burst alive with energy, stirring the crew to prepare for docking. At long last, the moment had arrived: he stepped one foot at a time down the plank. Like trumpets welcoming him, he felt solid earth under his feet and rejoiced; a surge of exhilaration swept through his body and he breathed in the air of land once more. It had never been so inviting.

He glanced around the wharf to sailors moseying about, sitting around to jokes or smoking; with the docks closed to trade there was little they could do but pass the day as they pleased. Leopaln started off when he bumped into a man shouldering a crate. His filthy clothes and stench could have easily mistaken him for a vagabond. "Watch where you're stepping!" the man snapped, upbraiding him with a crooked glare. "You mind where you're walking."

Leopaln contemplated apologizing, but then thought better of it. Given the sentiment of the colonies, weakness might only be exploited. Suddenly, the sailor put the crate down and called out behind him. "Hey Mobsy! Catch a whiff of something," he said, inhaling a deep breath. "I'd say it be another fool. Another filthy redcoat in the colonies, and another dead one." He laughed heartedly. "But I'll be, he's an officer. Well how do you reckon that? I ought to be more respectable shouldn't I," he said, letting loose another laugh. "Would you believe it Mobsy? An officer. I figured some pretty lass would walk by me today, but not an officer. Now how about that."

Everyone started laughing, and Mobsy strode over to Leopaln. His height and bulky barrel frame towered over the young officer, who had to look up to see his face; he was toned and intimidating to behold and his reed pipe hanging from his mouth only made him look that more daunting. He stopped short, stared at him and without turning his gaze grabbed onto the shoulder of the sailor who had called over to him. "A thousand apologies from this miscreant. He's unfamiliar with proper etiquette." The sailor screamed out in agony as Mobsy's hand dug into his shoulder. "Begging your pardon, but my acquaintance here is trying to say something and I reckon I can't make it out too well. One minute if you will." He squeezed even harder. "Now then, how do we greet the uniform?"

The man begged for mercy, but his pleas fell on deaf ears. With another harsh squeeze though he finally capitulated. "With respect. With respect!" he said, and Mobsy let him go. The lofty sailor then traced Leopaln from head to toe, summing him up. He wore a fine regiment coat of standard military red that extended down to his thighs with two small pockets on either side, and along its length were stitched sterling gold buttons displaying the royal seal of His Majesty: a crown staged in the foreground of a shield bearing the three islands of Jhor.

Upon his shoulders set a pair of epaulets and a fine officer's hat fit neatly upon his head. Underneath his coat, he wore a red waistcoat and a white shirt that still clung to the smell of the sea; below his waist he wore white breeches and polished black shoes. Upon his back he wore a knapsack.

Mobsy glared unkindly at him. As much as he detested the uniform he was not above paying respect to it. Just because Parliament had enacted a blockade and quartered soldiers into homes were not enough to persuade his allegiance towards independence; he was neither a radical calling for more rights nor an agitator, propagating open war with one of the strongest militaries of the day. He was a man of self-restraint, and proud to be a colonial citizen of one of the greatest powers on earth.

"You'll have to excuse him sir," Mobsy said apologizing on behalf of his ignorant shipmate. "He doesn't know how to treat an officer. My name is Eric "Mobsy" Fletcher, but the lads just call me Mobsy. I'm first-mate of that there ship, *The Crimson Queen*, and best believe it when I say it be a hell' of a ship. And these are my lads," he said, taking out his pipe and motioning it towards a handful of sailors. "They're as ignorant as rock on land, but on the open sea they're fine sailors; wouldn't find a wiser bunch. Isn't that right lads?" he said, as they let loose a cheer.

Meanwhile, as Leopaln stood steadfast in the face of the affronts, retaining the courtesy of a gentleman, he rummaged through his mind for the identity of the man's accent. It wasn't that of Jhor, but then neither was the man's attire or mannerisms: he smelled of salt and his clothes were dull from overuse; his regard for authority was as doubtful as his courtesy, and Leopaln wasn't sure whether to welcome his presumed allegiance or be wary of it.

The man was bulky, and from his breath he was a strong drinker, not out of ill habit but more likely for regaling with the derelicts of society. He had a short, red beard perched on his chin, which was a fiery inferno of a smelting furnace to the pale color of his white skin; surely his temper matched his color. And upon his head sat a cocked sailor's cap that covered his bird's nest wisp of uncombed red hair.

"And if you don't mind me asking," Mobsy asked, rather impolitely, "to where are you headed? Perhaps my lads and I can help you. We always try to do our best and treat officers right." His accent was Maerlic. Leopaln recognized it. It was from the third isle of Jhor on its western coast.

The Maerlese were of a clan's descent, strong-knit and highly distrustful of foreigners, if not their own. Rural and fierce, they had resisted Jhor's conquest for nearly four centuries, but when they had allied against the Crown they were finally undone; their lands were confiscated and many were forced to seek new fortunes in the New World; Mobsy's father had taught him how to sail and how to harbor enmity to old enemies.

"You know," he said, suddenly feeling the Maerlese hatred awaken within him. "I ain't ever killed an officer. A pity I didn't get my chance a few months back; though I reckon if the opportunity presented itself, I would certainly welcome it." He narrowed his glare at the officer and took a step closer; he meant to inflict injury, but something within him refrained his hands. "I don't like picking on fellows smaller than me," he said, storing away his animosity. "It just isn't civilized." As much as his father's voice shouted inside of his head, he refused to let the hatred win; he was Maerlese by blood, but a sailor by profession. His crew looked to him for setting the example.

"Sadly, you'd hardly put up a good scuffle my little officer," he said, bidding him a farewell. "Oh well lads, perhaps a taller fool will land tomorrow, and we'll have ourselves a good time." But as he turned away, the first sailor suddenly leapt at Leopaln, grabbing the nearest object he could find. "Jhor should send men to fight, not boys like you!" he said, raising the object over his head. "You're a bloody redcoat and I'm gonna crack your skull wide open!"

All at once, Leopaln froze. His training had taught him to react, but he found himself unable to do so; he meant to block the attack, but he knew it was too late. In a split second he would be hit. But just then Mobsy's strong arm knocked the sailor down. "You stand up and I'll put you down again!" he said, pointing directly at the man. All at once, his crew was gazing at him, stunned and amazed. A Maerlese had just defended a redcoat.

"Back to work," he ordered, sending them away without explanation of his actions; his own father was turning in his grave. Mobsy could hear the old dog shouting at him in his head; he had just dishonored his entire people. "Now you listen and you listen well," he said, pointing his finger at Leopaln. "You are not welcomed here, nor are you wanted here. Sail back to Jhor and tell them that it's going to take everything they have to keep these colonies from being independent, because there's more than enough of us Maerlese here. Now I just saved your arse, but I swear if Jhor wants blood than I won't be so merciful next time. And just so you hear it from me. Welcome to Clarkstown."

Chapter 3

Clarkstown

Whatever trumpeting welcome Leopaln imagined was now completely gone. The reality of the colonies was now fully apparent as he hadn't noticed until just then that his hands were trembling and his heart was racing. As Mobsy and his crew walked away, he glanced around in hopes of seeing something more appealing, but all he received were foul glares; sailors moseyed about or sat lazily about, passing the day with little care. Few if any were doing any actual work, which only served as a constant reminder of the blockade.

Leopaln stepped off the wharf and onto a wide brick street that housed empty warehouses and stores. Everywhere, folk were about, talking and gossiping; with little business to be had they instead occupied their time fomenting agitation and spreading rumors against the crown; not all businesses were dry however, but those belonged to loyalists and few if any with rebel sentiments wished to do   business with them.

To one side of the street looked out to the wharf, while at the other end sat simple brick buildings; unable to pay rent, many merchants had taken to the street with their goods in a wagon, selling what little they had left. Leopaln passed by many, amazed at how they hadn't lost their spirits; they were as proud as ever in fact, and often managed to pull some loiters about them just for conversation's sake.

"So, how's life?" asked the merchant. The other man smirked, "are you asking in hopes that mine is better than yours, or in hopes that I can make yours sound better than mine?" The two men laughed. Further up, Leopaln caught another group in the midst of their conversation.

"Damn this blockade is all I have to say, and I doubt any of would disagree," said one disgruntled colonial.

"Aye, what does Jhor expect to accomplish with it? My brother just returned from his brother-in-law's over there and said the man is hurting; he can't run his business without our lumber. I tell you, Parliament is nothing but halfwits and dolts."

A third man said his piece then. "The fact is we have legitimate grievances, but neither that ninny on the throne or Parliament will listen. First they impose taxes on us without representation from our colonial legislatures and when we ask for a proper voice they impose more taxes and this blockade. I can't sell anything now and they want me to sit on my arse all day and respect them. It's unfounded and outrageous!"

A ways up, Leopaln saw a man punch another to the ground. The man standing cursed his opponent and spit on him. When Leopaln hesitantly asked a bystander, the colonial replied coldly, "That man's a southerner. They're ports are still open as are their big mouths."

Further up the street, Leopaln listened to artisan-venders bellow their voices into the air, selling as proudly as if they still owned brick and mortar. "Fish for sale, nothing fresher than fresh fish!" "Beautiful pottery, beautiful colors, see for yourself!" "Cloth, gorgeous cloth. Buy for the lady!" When he passed by the fish vender, Leopaln pinched his nose. The grotesque smell of rotting fish was appalling, but apparently the man didn't notice as he picked up another, removed its head, tore out the guts and fileted it.

Leopaln was on Wharf Street, and everyone he passed either pretended to ignore him or issued him an unsettling glare. One deranged man, hunched over with an eye patch, pushed his way through the bustling just to spit on him. As Leopaln wiped his coat, his patience wore thin; first it was Mobsy and then the cold welcoming stares and now this loony spitting on him. He suddenly wished for the sea over Clarkstown.

He knew the office he was to report to, but not how to get there. He was about to ask for directions, but thought better of it; beggars were treated better than he it seemed, and in fact he followed a few. After all, who else might know how to evade the law than those living on the street?

He crossed alley and street, passing by brick buildings that he recognized, realizing then that he was going in circles. He doubled-back and crossed another street, but found himself lost time and again; at least being lost was better than the fate of some beggars, who were mercilessly beaten with walking sticks by those taking out their reproach of Jhor on those in destitute; to be reminded by the pauper was far worse than being stung by the air: at least gossip had a tendency to be embellished.

Leopaln avoided eye contact, but his presence was hardly inescapable. His uniform drew uneasy stares, and he couldn't help but feel he was being watched at every turn; paranoia gripped at him and he soon worried that everyone gossiping was pointing him out. Wherever he went, heads turned towards him, especially women, who shot him such resentful stares that he felt inclined to believe their looks were far more imposing than the full might of Jhor.

At best, he was outnumbered by a city that resented his presence. But at last, he saw his destination and hastened his step. It was a three-story brick building with four sentries standing post outside; security was an unquestionable necessity. They came to attention and offered a salute as he approached; one opened the door for him and warned him to mind his step inside. And surely enough, Leopaln took one step in and was greeted by chaos. Everywhere, people were shuffling by, moving frantically about as if hysteria had possessed the building. Papers were on the floor and covering desks; the occupancy was clearly trying to keep up with a calamity that refused to slow down. Even hallways were busied with trunks stacked to the ceiling, and staff squeezing by. Leopaln had no idea where to go, but picked a corridor and went down it.

"Damn, damn, damn!" shouted a voice from within a room. He was clearly of high rank and seated behind his desk, frustrated beyond belief. He was filling out an uninterrupted flow of paperwork that he hardly noticed Leopaln standing in his doorway. "You, get in here. The rest of you, get out! I said out! Now!" His staff insisted on the workload, but he didn't care. "Frankly, I don't give a rat's arse how soon His Majesty needs it. It can wait five minutes dammit!" He motioned to Leopaln. "You, get in here!"

"I'm sorry sir, I just arrived," Leopaln said, nervously entering   the   room.

"Well, that's obvious," the man said. "And I bet you got a warm welcome. Filthy sack of loony-bunches carrying

33

pitchforks and waving independence in our face; they're making more trouble for me than the godforsaken natives," he said, referring to the recent encounters by colonials pioneers disobeying the law and encroaching onto native lands. "It's a clear act of disobedience, but what can you expect. Apparently, we live in a world where rules are bent, not obeyed. Bloody colonials."

Leopaln looked puzzled. He hadn't heard about the encroaching. "Forget about it," the man said. "Just give me your papers and I'll assign your post." At that moment though, several heads popped in his doorway. "Dammit, what did I just say? Get out of here!" Then he issued a prayer to his ceiling. "Dear Lord, give me the strength to survive this day... so I can drink it off tonight."

Then turning back to Leopaln he reviewed his papers, signed them and returned them to him along with some additional paperwork. "Go to our building on 11th Street. Now pay attention. To get there, walk three blocks south and then take 6th Street. That will take you right into 11th St."

Leopaln stuffed his papers inside his jacket and started for the door. "Lieutenant," the man called out. "Aren't you forgetting something?" Apologizing, Leopaln turned and saluted him. Then he hustled outside as the commandant resumed his barking.

The Nations: Fraternity

As he stepped outside, he pulled out his papers and reviewed them. Something wasn't quite right, but orders were orders and he wanted to get to his next destination as quickly as possible. And so, he stuffed the papers back into his jacket and headed off. At 6th Street, he turned and his nose immediately objected to the street's filthy stench of manure; apparently sailors weren't the only ones not working. Nevertheless, he thought 6th St. to be an improvement of even Wharf St. The architecture was much more ascetically appealing, and there were more loyalists about; it was no secret that 6th St. was loyalist, hence its nickname, Six for Sticks, referring to the fact that those with walking sticks were presumably loyalists since they could still afford Jhor's high prices.

He passed by a vender selling cloth and bought some yellow color for her. He knew she would love it when he returned. Just then a strong breeze swept by, and he clutched his coat tightly. Unfortunately, the putrid stench of manure caught his nose and he hurried off to the nearest building and let himself in. It was a bookstore, and all at once he was reminded of his father's library. Suddenly, his eyes wandered, wondering if this place had his favorite book. He shifted down the aisles, staring at the covers, and hoping he might find it. At long last, he found it; the memories of reading it in his father's library came rushing back. Slowly, he opened it.

In the days of old, when darkness covered all the lands, a withering soul was dispatched from its eternal imprisonment, and set forth upon a mission. It wandered the mountains and forests and river-towns, searching out a man; a mortal that could lift the darkness and bring rejoice back to the lands. For the soul had been told to do so by the master, a darkness of the ancients, and indisputably, it believed the master. Though had it any sense of mind it would have reasoned and turned back. But such was not to be. And at long last, it found Him. There on a hilltop, standing like a giant among Men, His banner raised high to the sky, and He shouted with all His might, so as to shake the earth and every mortal creature within ear. It should not have chosen Him, but it did.

Leopaln closed the book and set out again. The breeze outside had eased and now the warm sun on him felt good. As he continued onward he failed to notice three unsavory men approach him from behind; they had spotted him through the bookstore window and were intent on exacting some revenge. All at once they grabbed him and threw him into an alley; he stumbled but tried to rise until a foot met his stomach. The letter from her from fell out of his pocket and they reached for it. Mockingly, they read it and laughed. "Give it back you thieves," he ordered, but they only ignored him; although he was reeling in pain, he could tell they hadn't bathed in awhile. The stench was undeniable.

As Leopaln tried to recover, intent on putting an end to the charade of humiliation, one of the vagabonds kicked him again. "You stay down redcoat friend," he shouted. "Best keep you're mouth shut too." But with each sentence he read of her words, Leopaln felt his patience thin even more; anger consumed him. He had tried to be a gentleman, but the provocations he had endured were intolerable; her words had restrained him, reminding him to rise above the depravity, but as the man mocked her sweet words he couldn't help but tighten his fist. "I said, give it back!"

"Oh, you want this," the man said, ripping the letter in half. "Oh so sorry." But just as Leopaln was about to rush him a fist to his temple knocked him to the ground. When he came to the men were long gone and his letter lay in mud; a calm gust of wind brushed against his face and sent a shiver down his battered body. He hated this place, and taking both halves he tucked them into his knapsack and continued onwards; the men hadn't taken anything else fortunately.

Setting back onto 6th Street, he lifted his chin and minded his step more cautiously. He only stopped once to buy another piece of cloth that he felt she might enjoy also; he was now wary of everyone and trusted no one. At 11th St., he rounded the corner and came to a sudden halt. All at once, his mouth dropped and his eyes widened at the unimaginable sight before him; he had neither expected to see such a sight nor something so bustling as what lay in front of him. All over, hundreds of colonials went about their day, gossiping, trading, discussing politics, or taking a reprieve to enjoy a meal; if Wharf Street was busy then 11th St. was a metropolis. As he quickly discovered, it was 11th St. that was the heart of the city.

All over, people sat around reading the newspaper, talking or visiting stores. Business was booming, largely for its service to both loyalist and rebel alike, but more so for its proliferation of goods offered as well as its lack of prejudice towards its clientele; in addition to offering every necessity or luxury, including local farm produce, politics also ran deep here as did the pockets of soldiers, who found the welcoming atmosphere more conducive to their spending habits and as far as the merchants of 11th St. were concerned that was good enough for their purses. The more patriotic agitators called them traitors, but they referred to themselves as simply good businessmen.

And unlike Wharf St., 11th St. ran amuck with various tongues. Most spoke the language of Jhor, but there were also others like Maerlic and those from Bahn and Romennal. At any given time, 11th St. was alive with the tongues of world languages, giving it truly the feeling of a major port-city. Even the colonials had their own variation of certain words, which were uncommon in Jhor; often the spelling was different, although the meaning was the same. The renaming of words was just one-way colonial agitators passively resisted Jhor, but another was the refusal to fly her flag; 11th St. had more foreign banners flying than her mother country.

Leopaln walked onto 11th St., mesmerized by the endless shops, apartments above and too many taverns to count. He passed by a butcher shop with a sign that read, "Only the Finest Meats Around," and at its doorway an elderly man sat reading the newspaper, licking his finger as he turned each page. The man spotted the young officer and tipped his hat respectfully.

Further on stood city hall with its two stone volute pillars, aged but still resolute as a symbol of authority; its legislative vacancy by order of Parliament did nothing to shake its prowess however, fueling the discontent further instead of quieting it. And although the flag of Jhor waved from its rooftop it was more of an obligation than a matter of pride. Leopaln took a pause to read a newspaper. He felt the need to sit down and after the morning he had endured the feeling was greatly welcomed:

VICTORY. Despite early setbacks of defeat against Romennal, His Majesty's army has emerged triumphant. And after six months of besiegement, the great port-city of Voggénlor has been captured. Throughout Jhor, sanguine cheers resound to the heroes of this colossal   victory.

In addition, His Majesty's armies, under the overall command of
Lord Horwick, have left the farming fields of Romennal in utter
despair. And with the capture of Voggénlor, Lord Horwick has
expressed confidence to Parliament that Romennal will soon seek
terms   of   peace.

Despite the loss of their great port-city, however, there are several
reports that Romennal will continue fighting. Yet, with its fields
ruined, its trade impeded and armies reduced it is only a matter of
time   before   this   conflict   is   concluded.

Leopaln was pleased to hear that. He had several friends
serving with Lord Horwick and wished them a safe farewell
when they departed nearly a year ago; he hoped they were doing
well still. He continued on for another block where he found the
building he was looking for. Strangely, it was unguarded. Letting
himself inside, he found the door unlocked and not even a
sentry within.

Inside hung a large chandelier, illuminating the foyer, but
adjoining rooms were left to the mercy of whatever sunlight
pierced through its unwashed windows; the air was quiet and
stagnant; none of the windows were open, and in fact none had

been for some time. It was as unwelcoming of a place as one that time forgot. "Hello, sir," said an attendant, suddenly into the room and startling Leopaln. "Please, wait here." Then, the man went down a hallway, and disappeared around the corner. While he waited, Leopaln looked for a place to sit, but the only chairs in the room looked unpleasantly uncomfortable and so he stood.

The room was barren, to say the least, apart from the chestnut bookcase at one end, which was filled with an assortment of classics and a bust of a historical figure that was indiscernible. He stepped closer to see if he might recognize it, but just then the attendant returned. "If you'll follow me, sir." The two went up a flight of stairs, where a sentry greeted them. Leopaln was told to wait again, as the attendant went on ahead to the door at the end of the hall. Knocking as if in code, he entered, said a few words and then returned to Leopaln. "You may follow me now." Whoever the commandant was, thought Leopaln, he was certainly a man of secrecy and caution. Even the building exterior had bore no sign of Jhor, not even a flag.

Chapter 4

Chapter 4

William Rogers

"Leopaln! My old friend," said a familiar voice as he entered. "Welcome. Welcome, my dearest friend." The man rejoiced in seeing him. "How have you been, and how have you come to be in this room? Assigned, reassigned or may I presume you are unaware to the answers of these questions. Oh, it is a pleasure to see you." The man had an enormous smile about him. "You seem in such high spirits, save for the fact that you look terrible. Did you get into a quarrel of some kind? And you tore your coat. I shall have my secretary send this for repair. Please, please, sit. Be comfortable. And by the by, would you like some tea?" he said, starting to pour some for himself. Leopaln thanked him as he took it. "When did you arrive?"

"Just this morning."

"This morning?" he said surprised. "Surely, it must have been some adventure then!"

"Indeed," he said, setting his tea down, "but before sharing my tale though, I must admit the hospitality of this city is breathtaking. In no manner does Clarkstown bereave a man of his dignity, nor his self-worth. Quite the opposite in truth, and to speak benevolently, I had women embrace me with hugs and kisses to the cheek the minute I stepped off the ship, and if I recall, 'Thank you kind sir, for defending our beloved city of Clarkstown against the ruthless dogs that so terribly bite at us. Indeed, truth to the last word I speak, I swear," he said sarcastically. "And in taverns! In there, I sat amongst Clarkstown's most audacious sailors, listening to their fabricated tales of sea voyages as we all drank to our dainty delight. Why, I've never felt this safe since I left Jhor three months ago." His friend nearly rolled over with laughter.

"Truly, you are something of a character, Leopaln," he replied happily. "I'll confess you haven't lost your sense of humor. Drinking to our dainty delight! Good Heavens, if nothing else Jhor sent you here to laugh the rebels into submission." He took a sip of his own tea. "Heavens, I certainly have missed you, and our days at the academy. Leopaln, my old friend, it has been far too long." Leopaln nodded in agreement. "But honestly, I had not expected to receive you. Be it you of course, of all officers of Jhor, who appears before my door in these dire hours. Though, I cannot imagine who else it may have been. Drinking to our dainty delight- oh gracious me- if laughter was the cure to war we'd be a happier race of men. Would you not agree?"

"Quite, but then what of us? If man did not conduct war, you nor I would be a soldier, so what then, what would you do then?" he said, enticing his friend's imagination.

"If I were not a soldier, mmm. A perplexing thought I must admit," he said, thinking about that. "Well, I see myself as a politician, like my father intended. He would have preferred my career be spent handling the affairs of state instead of over here, but then I suppose we strengthen His Majesty's realm by doing this just as well. After all, are we not builders of a greater dream? I would say so. Now what of you? What would you be?"

Leopaln thought for a second. "You ask me truthfully, but how can I speak honestly when you have not done so yourself. You think I have forgotten you, but I know better. You never wanted to be a politician."

He became theatrical. "Leopaln, I am heart-stricken you do not believe me. To think, after all the years we spent together at the academy and before. A pox on you," he said, but then burst into laughter, unable to contain himself any longer. "You know me too well! I could not hold it back any longer. Truly you are a gift from Heaven at my doorstep; may Heaven shine graciously upon you, for you truly have not forgotten me. Oh gracious me, I must admit politics is definitely not for me. Politics suits my father fine, but not me. Though, one cannot blame politics for the problems of man," he said. "It is the character of man that provokes it."

"This is true."

"Therefore, and without further ado," he said, "I solemnly admit defeat and relinquish my sword to you, and ask benevolently, if you will tell your tale for I long to hear it."

"I shall do so," agreed Leopaln, "but let me first return to your earlier observation, for it does pertain to my account of arriving in Clarkstown? Indeed this city's hospitality is not of the sort I expected, but rather lingering in the gutter. For instance, the second I set foot onto the wharf I was greeted by its foulness, and it left me wondering why there are no sentries posted on Wharf Street, or for that matter why few are about in the city, do you know why?"

"Yes, but please continue." And so Leopaln regaled him with his stories of that morning, of Mobsy, Wharf Street, the barking commandant, the scuffle on 6th Street and his overall reflection of the city itself.

"And so that is my tale," he said, "which now brings me to my earlier inquiry of before. Why are there few sentries or even patrols in this city? Surely, I would have expected the opposite. What explains this absence, William?"

His friend nodded, but suddenly became serious, as though overtaken by some notion or grave thought. For a minute he sat silently, discerning how best to answer the question. Finally, he spoke. "I'm certainly not that high up, but I do know a thing or two of what's going on here, and I agree I would personally prefer to see more patrols out. Unfortunately, the answer to your question has many, and so let me start with one. Rebellion is everywhere. It's in the south, the central colonies, and here in the north as well. But fortunately colonial politics have a way of preventing collaboration and for the moment that plays in our favor.

He leaned in, his tone serious. "I have an entire arsenal to end the rebellion tomorrow, but with the war abroad and insurrection everywhere I do not have the necessary manpower; some buildings in the city have one sentry, such as my own. Others, such as the one you were at earlier, have more. We are reluctantly doing more with less."

"Is this arsenal guarded," Leopaln asked, troubled by what his friend was saying. "After all, from the way you make is sound it certainly must house enough munitions to warrant interest of any particular parties."

"As the quartermaster, I can tell you there is more than enough munitions, but I can say no more."

"And of the insurrection? It is getting worse?"

"Indeed, and unfortunately Parliament is to thank for much of that. They do not have as keen of an understanding of how things operate here in the colonies as I do and you will soon have. In terms of laws, one cannot simply pass a law and expect men to change, especially those that might already have a constitution that is less than cooperative, such as this unsavory sailor you met this morning.

"What works back home unfortunately doesn't work here, largely owing to the fact that there is an ocean between the lawmaker and the citizen; one simply cannot expect obedience with two thousand miles in between. And to say these colonials have representation is foolhardy, especially when a representative has neither set foot here nor is from here. But please, don't mistake me. I am not for these colonials, but I do try to understand the dynamics of the circumstances that I find myself a part of."

Leopaln raised a hopeful smile. "Fortunately, the war abroad is nearing an end," he said. "And I expect we will shortly be able to buy their wares again. I do miss Romennal wine." He hoped a bit of light humor might lighten the conversation.

"My father enjoys it too, but then who doesn't? Of course, if war does anything for civilization then I believe it builds respect among nations. I would certainly rather be over there in Romennal than here behind this desk."

"I'd rather be behind that desk, and you would stay if you had my morning."

"I have had your morning, everyday since I arrived," William said, smiling faintly as though hiding something. "We are vulnerable, Leopaln, more than may know. The war abroad has created a shortage of officers and depleted our manpower that any catalyst here will prove disastrous to the realm; hear me well, old friend, we are sitting on the verge of calamity. We are more vulnerable than you could possibly imagine.

"For the moment, everything is calm, but the storm is brewing. It beckons, and I promise you when it happens we will be undone; we have the rivers patrolled and sentries about, but it will not be enough. When these colonies rebel in full spirit, and they will, there will be nothing to stop them. Be assured, as much as Romennal is suffering so too are we, only Parliament hasn't realized it yet. You have my sincere apologies old friend for being so dismal, but there is little I can do to comfort you in this place except to be honest."

Leopaln nodded. He appreciated his friend's candor, and gestured him to continue. "To wit," William added, "I have received a letter from my superior granting me authority and jurisdiction over the City of Clarkstown. It is highly unusual, given my standing, but owing to my duties and the subsequent few officers there are in the colonies, particularly here, I am both honored and resentful. It puts a tremendous burden of responsibility on me, particularly when I lack the necessary manpower to enforce martial law.

"Without adequate resources and staff, my ability to preserve law and order is inevitably flawed. I have half the officers I need, a few sentries and patrols and to make matters worse the Guard Advice, the pinnacle of our non-commissioned ranks, have been acting adversely since they are continuously put in harm's way, which I cannot blame them, but I have no alternative.

"And yet to compound this already growing dilemma, I have superiors that expect impractical results and in exchange I get assurances and promises that are unreliable at best… to stress my honesty, I was informed that a detachment was arriving and instead I got you. I am not disappointed by the company," he snickered, trying to save face, "but by the frugality of command. Apparently, you and I are expected to put down a rebellion if that's what happens."

Leopaln shared his laugh. He was not offended, and so his friend continued. "If the rebellion resurfaces, overcomes the southern defenses, or our northern ones, then it is only a matter of time. The patrols we have along the Rapid River in the central region will only buy us some time. But whatever the case, we will not have enough to quell an uprising. Now I don't mean to worry you outright," he added. "Clarkstown has defenses as do other cities. We do have forts and garrisons, but a protracted conflict is what I foresee being the colonial strategy; we cannot endure a war of attrition with such limited supplies. Even that arsenal I spoke of will become depleted over time."

William leaned back in his chair then. He was pleased to have an old friend's company, but the gravity of the situation concerned him; he cared for Leopaln and worried for his wellbeing. "Might I see your papers?"

Leopaln handed them over, William read them carefully, but suddenly sat upright. Flipping back and forth he couldn't believe what he was reading. "It says you have been placed in command of an entire company. And while I congratulate you, it is certainly a rarity for a lieutenant." He raised an eyebrow. "I wonder if your father played a role in that?" Leopaln hoped that wasn't the case, but he certainly didn't dismiss it; anything was possible with his father's connections. But William went on, reading the orders further. "It says your company will secure the roads as far north as Clarkstown and as far south as Devonshire." A look of puzzlement crossed his face. "But that's already being patrolled. Why would we need two patrols on it, especially given our depleted state? It makes no sense."

The Nations: Fraternity

"I don't understand it either," Leopaln said, prompting his friend to reach for a map of the colonies. They cleared the desk and laid it out and William explained his worry.

"Here is Devonshire, lying southwest of us and between either of these two cities is Sterling Road. Now it's about a week's march between either with villages and towns running in between, but the area has had no reports of incident. So, why would you be assigned this, and for what purpose would require an entire company?

"To be perfectly honest, I'm rather puzzled as well hesitant to dispatch an entire company away from the city, especially when Devonshire is far smaller than Clarkstown."

He moved his finger across the map. "Your assignment is to secure all these roads including Sterling Road, but I know for certain they are unthreatened; the only reports of disturbances are of bandits, which are mostly reported by bickering drunkards hoping for a sympathetic coin to come his way and then off to the tavern the imbecile goes."

"Could it be rebel sympathies?"

"Not likely," William said, bemused by this enigma. "Right now, reports only indicate that the rebels have moved south, and as I said before the rivers are now being watched as are key strategic points; to attempt anything would only alert us." He took another sip of tea.

There were too many questions and not enough answers, and despite being a captain he had little pull; information was as scarce as manpower these days. "It is the simplest understanding to me that perhaps you are not to secure the road itself, but something on the road. But then what might that be?"

"Munitions perhaps?"

"No, certainly not that," he said, setting the tea down. "I would be the first to know if that were the case. Besides, there is a current restriction of arms in public; anyone found carrying or concealing will have their firearm confiscated. We cannot be too careful these days. Everyone is potentially a sympathizer for the rebellion."

"Then perhaps it is nothing more than deterrence," Leopaln offered. "After all, any show of strength would impress upon others considering insurrection."

"Possibly," he admitted. "That is indeed a possibility. And so I say let that be the reason, at least for now," he said, shifting the conversation. "It is as compelling of any reason as I can deduce myself, and so let us leave it at that; whether it be that or something else, let us simply resolve to discover the truth at a future date; to partake in presumptions would only waste our time together catching up, and so let us speak of other matters."

Leopaln smiled, happy to oblige. "I would enjoy that very much," he said. "So please tell me of your adventures since the academy? I long to hear them."

"Adventures with paperwork is more like it," he laughed. But his glee was suddenly and without warning purloined by a translucent melancholy that all at once crossed his face and ensnared him, supplanting his happiness for something grave and serious. It was as though he had remembered something sad and misfortunate.

Leopaln cleared his throat in hopes of stirring his friend, but alas he remained steadfast in his silence and gloom; whatever had shaken him was doing a splendid job in arresting his recovery to happier thoughts. Even a joke was unable to resurrect him. "Tell me what vexes you, old friend, for whatever it is you must cast it aside and remember that a friend is with you, and if you cannot return then I will plunge your feather pen into my heart so as to give you a reason for sorrow. Though I can't quite imagine the terrible difficulty it will be to pierce my skin I shall nevertheless find a way."

To his great triumphant, the captain returned. "A thousand apologies," he said, recovering himself. "I was lost in my thoughts and your offer of sacrifice was as foolish as it was enough to return me. Good heavens, you are indeed a good friend, Leopaln. A feather pen, seriously of all things, you would choose that?" he said, laughing.

"The simple things in life."

"Ha, indeed! Truly, you are a great friend, Leopaln and I thank you for entertaining my sadness away. You must forgive my leave, I did not mean to. Humorous men like you I swear."

"Please I beg no trophies just answers to questions, and if I may, I wish to inquire of what we spoke earlier. A thought occurred to me," he said, returning to the map. "Might I inquiry as to what travels between the two cities, particularly on Sterling Road? Is it civilians, commercial goods, or military personnel?"

"An excellent inquiry," said the captain, feeling life return into his soul; work kept his mind occupied from the thoughts that he kept bottled. "And in fact, I have such an answer." Retrieving a logbook, he brought it over to the desk. "As quartermaster, I'm responsible or not only munitions and equipment, but also all personnel entering or leaving the city limits, civilian and military; with martial law enacted here, it is vital to know who is traversing and the business they carry between locations.

Shortly after the initial skirmishes, only military personnel and civilians with signed papers were allowed access between cities; limiting passage was a precautionary measure to protect our supply wagons, as you can well understand. So alluding to my earlier assumption that you might be protecting something besides the road, I suspect it might be a convoy."

"A convoy of goods, munitions or personal?"

He scanned the logbook. "I'm not sure. According to the recent entries, there is a shipment being delivered to the garrison at Devonshire?"

"That must be it then."

"I suspect so, but still it doesn't explain the coincidence of your command and the dispatch of an entire company to that location. Do you think your father played a role in that?"

"Let's not speak of him," he said.

"My father and yours are friends too. Certainly, there is as much of a future ahead of us as our fathers intend; we cannot escape destiny, Leopaln."

"Perhaps, but I wish to believe I have some say in the matter."

"Against the will of your father? You do know who the man is right?"

"I know who my father is, William," he said irate at the insinuation. "I don't need to be reminded."

"Then you know there is a good chance that he had some say. I mean, after all, what lieutenant gets command of an entire company? Good gracious, I'm behind a desk and I outrank you!"

"I should be off," Leopaln said, uncomfortable with the notion that his father influenced his orders. "It was a pleasure to see you, old friend."

William tried to apologize. "I didn't mean to offend, but I understand you need to get going. But you know what I'm saying is probably true."

"Please William, say no more."

"You really hate him, don't you?"

"I respect him. There's a difference."

William snickered. "He's one of the most powerful men in the world and you're probably the only person who can actually hurt him."

"It was good to see you too," he said, not amused.

"Alright, I'll send for the carriage."

"To where?"

"Fort Heritage. It's only a few miles away, but perhaps we should have lunch first."

"I would enjoy that," Leopaln said, accepting the invitation. "And will anyone else be joining us? Any other friends of ours from the academy?"

Once again, silence took the room as William looked away, staring out the window onto 11th St. His glare narrowed to those passing by and despite all attempts by Leopaln to retract him, the sorrow refused to retreat; the pain was too great, and like a shroud of plague enveloping an unprotected populace, he too felt infected, only willingly. He allowed the sorrow and misery to canopy him, bereave him of all hope and life, and tear at him with painful memories of those lost, stolen in the prime of their life; what friends they had were now gone, or were certainly destined to be buried.

What torture was this to happen Leopaln to him at this hour? Surely, the Devil wasn't satisfied with taking his soul. Now he meant to taunt him as well; he did not know the circumstances of those friends fighting in Romennal, but he knew the fates of those that had come to the colonies, and he could not bring himself to share it with Leopaln. They were all gone, perished in the opening days of the rebellion.

Of all those who came before, only Leopaln remained alive and for certain his days were numbered, thought William, turning solemnly; the tremendous grief of losing yet another pained him grievously. Surely, his days were numbered too, but then who would go first.

"I am departed," he said, admitting his sadness but saying no more: he wished to tell him, but he could not. Leopaln was all he had left, and to break his heart with such news would be unbearable. "What has come… and what will be," he finally said, his voice trailing off. And with that, he called for his attendant to ready the carriage. There would be no lunch.

Chapter 5

In Company with the Guard Advice

Standing in the doorway of the foyer, Leopaln hesitated to leave his friend, but the carriage had arrived and he needed to be on his way. Whatever despondency ailed his friend was proving unbearable; he wondered what he could do to help, if anything. As the attendant tried to assure him that the captain's wellbeing was being cared for a thunderous crash suddenly came from upstairs. At once, Leopaln rushed back inside and peeked his head over the stairwell banister; had he heard something, or was it just his imagination? He waited a few seconds, but there was only silence.

As he slowly turned away he heard a soft wailing drift down the stairwell, obliging him to pause momentarily and listen. Steadily, the sobs became louder, and Leopaln could hear the captain's voice cry out in pain; whatever had him was refusing to let go like a choir of damned souls moaning eternally in agony. It was excruciating to listen to and Leopaln felt helpless; the attendant once again tried to assure him that his friend would be looked after, but what remedy was there for this? He was unsure. How could he leave his friend suffering so? Clearly, the man was in a state of irrevocable melancholy, but for what reason remained unknown.

"See to it that he's cared for," he finally said, acquiescing to the attendant's assurances. "I cannot bear to see an old friend this way." To abandon William was unthinkable, but he had no resolution to cure his affliction. "Be well, William," he said turning to the doorway. He didn't want to leave, but William was always strong, perhaps even stronger than he. Whatever ailed him, he could handle.

Outside the sun showered its warmth on the land. It felt good on the back of Leopaln's neck, and he paused to embrace it. His morning had been adventurous, to say the least, and he hoped for a more restful afternoon. Waiting at the curb was the carriage with the driver holding the door open for him. "Mind your step sir," the man said, closing it behind him. Then the carriage departed.

Inside, Leopaln was seated across two men who bid him welcome, but whereas one was an attendant of some sort, perhaps a sentry escort, the other appeared to be a guest from abroad. His foreign attire was undeniably distinct, particularly its design, which was more fashionable to that of Romennal not Jhor suggesting that he was either oblivious to his surroundings or was supremely confident in the protection he had been given; then again, with the colonial conditions as they were it seemed entirely possible that the man's attire was the least of anyone's concern.

His coat was purple and upon his breast he wore an array of decorated medals, signifying both his feats as well as someone of note, but it was his imperious aura about him that stood out, exuding experience and influence. He was a gentleman and no doubt from old wealth, but by the way he carried himself his inheritance had played only a secondary role in his achievements:

His face was aged, worn by perseverance and tragedy; he had endured at great expense, losing a wife and daughter at sea, but carrying on nevertheless in their memory. He honored them instead of mourning them, leveraging their memories to carry him forward each day, thanking them for allowing him to remember them in his way as he reshaped the world to make it a better place.

Leopaln greeted them kindly as they bid him welcome, but he could not resist feeling some apprehension about the foreigner, including some intimidation by the man's rigid facial expression which was masked by his trimmed imperial white beard. But the man nodded to him, offering a smile to ease the awkwardness. Nevertheless, Leopaln wondered about their purpose, and to what end they were headed in his same direction.

"You are inquisitive," said the foreigner. "I can see that." Leopaln nodded cautiously. "Well then, let me begin by introducing myself. I am the Marquis de Eliám, and it is a pleasure to meet you."

"You're not from Romennal, are you?" Leopaln asked, finding no other way to say it but being impolite. "I'm sorry, it's just that you-"

"That I look fashionably like someone from there," he said, interrupting him with a chuckle. "Quite so, but no. I am from the north, Aiegona to be exact."

"I did not realize Aiegona and Romennal were so similar in their fashions."

"Yes, indeed they are, but that is about all we share in common, lest I suffer the same fate as it appears you did since you've arrived," he said, noting the tear in his coat. "I see you've experienced some colonial disdain."

"Uh, yes, there were three of them," Leopaln said.

"Indeed there were," he said, with a latent nod, "but I can see you are a man resolved to carry on. Well done." Leopaln was surprised by that remark, but thanked him for the compliment. "I am a representative here on the affairs of my countrymen," the Marquis said, going on. "For some time our borders have enjoyed peace and prosperity, but with the recent contravention in your colonies it has fallen to me to ascertain the situation in a more personal manner; it seems your sovereignty and mine are of the mutual opinion that the preservation of the colonies is essential for commerce, and so that is my business here. I hope you don't mind the company?" Leopaln shook his head. "And by the by, please excuse the driver," he said, acknowledging Leopaln's subtle discomfort to the speed. "He insists on making good time; that or there is a storm coming."

The Marquis de Eliám was intent on his purpose, which was to yield Jhor in her theory that her domestic strife in the colonies was more than just insurgency. It was belligerency; despite the setback months earlier, the colonial agitators were only gaining strength, rallying more followers to the cause of independence. And while this was a domestic issue for Jhor, she had yet to quell it, troubling her neighbors who feared the repercussion of a new nation; the aged pact was now centuries old, more myth than law, but nevertheless no sovereignty on the continent dared to violate the venerable treaty for fear of what the others might do.

The Nations: Fraternity

Any secessionist movement therefore drew attention, particularly by how reckless the colonials were, from casting wares into the water to tarring and feathering tax collectors, declaring outwardly that taxation without representation was an abomination to rule without consent by blatantly ignoring the fact that they already had a voice in Parliament and furthermore paid no heed that their perfidious actions only aroused interest from their neighbors who could easily march into the colonies, at Jhor's blessing, and silence the agitators.

The Rights of Man, as they so boldly declared, were not inherent gifts, but the measure of one's actions in an imperfect world. Being a better person and making the world a better place weighed heavier than a man granted freedom at birth, for a man who does not know hardship couldn't appreciate the chains coming off. The Marquis knew this all too well. As a boy, he had seen the auction blocks. How could men sell other men? His youthful eyes had witnessed another child his age being sold to a man that whipped him publicly to stop him from resisting; the boy wanted freedom, but had to suffer first. And years later, the Marquis bought that young boy and gave him a proper life; the boy was his property, but the Marquis treated him as his equal, and now he rode with him in the carriage.

History of all things is imperfect, because it repeats itself, thought the Marquis. But it is the imperfections of society that result from the deficiencies from within; slavery was an abomination, and perhaps more so than the inherent Rights of Man, but the folly of humanity was also its greatest gift. Man learned, and while the Marquis did not completely embrace the colonial agitators, his manservant did; his name given to him was Nathaniel, but the Marquis often referred to him as Nate, and if seeing a gentlemen in Romennal fashion wasn't surprising enough nor even a colored manservant in the colors of Jhor than hearing a slave speak freely was even more daunting. Nate was permitted to speak his mind, and the Marquis insisted upon it. He valued Nate's insight, and granted him more liberties, not because it was his way of opposing the institution of slavery, but because Nate had suffered so much hardship that only now as a grown man did he appreciate the freedom the Marquis bestowed upon him.

Men dream of freedom, but only those in chains will ever value that freedom more than a man born into it. This was the Marquis's mantra. Men had to suffer first before being blessed; enduring tragedy was the cost of liberty, and although he was born into wealth, he had suffered like any other: only to death is Man equal, he thought, remembering his wife and daughter. He grieved for them everyday, but always carried himself forward and did all he could to make the world a better place, taking Nate with him wherever he went; where he had lost a best friend he had gained another.

Leopaln stared out the window. The sun shone brightly, but in the distance clouds gathered at the horizon. Surely, a great storm was coming, but he hoped it wouldn't last long. As a youth, he ran to his father, scared of the lightning and thunder; now he laughed. But his father had been there for him, and told him stories to help him sleep.

"Just as a storm may pass," he had said, "so will the troubles you will face some day."

"What troubles do you face each day?" he asked, hiding in his arms. His father smiled, "Many things, but I worry most about you. I want you to grow up and be stronger than me, and to ensure that I must labor everyday to make the world ready for you."

"You make the world go round?" he said innocently.

His father laughed. "Of course not, but in a way I do. The world is a big place, and filled with many people, some good and some bad, but it's men like me that help make the world a smaller place."

"How do you do that?"

"By working with others, Leopaln. There are many nations in this world, great nations, and sometimes we agree on things, and sometimes we don't."

"What happens when you don't agree?"

His father's face grew solemn. "When we don't agree bad things happen; things we often regret, but at the time we thought were necessary."

"Like what?"

His father hesitated. "We do horrible things to each other; it's what we call war, and it's something I hope to keep you from." He would say no more about it; war always cost more than what went on paper: peace was just a recess until the next major engagement, for neither Jhor, Romennal nor even Bahn, the third major power, were willing to permit another to amputate their hold over the world without a fight.

Leopaln remembered how his father would speak of this rivalry between nations as a contest between men and their characters. "There will always be quarrel in this world, Leopaln, because men always disagree; it is the one inherent flaw in our character, whether by our customs, language, or values. It is the one thing we can agree upon; that we will always disagree."

Had the Marquis ever met his father perhaps he too would have agreed. Conflict was both a curse upon humanity as it was a blessing, coercing men to either advance or be destroyed, and the recent skirmish between colonials and regulars was no exception; in addition to its ramifications reverberating in neighboring states as well as further beyond to nations such as Romennal, whose agents were now fomenting the clamor for independence in the colonies, it also challenged the values of brethren, if not kinship and blood. This clash between colonial and Jhor was more than a disagreement of principals. It was a struggle between how one group of individuals chose to advance itself: should it be guided as a parent holds a child's hand, or seize its own destiny and carve its own path into history?

And the Marquis was troubled by that thought, because even a newborn cannot be read. Would a new nation respect its neighbors or annex them? Would it succumb to blind ambition, conquering in the name of Life, Liberty and the Pursuit of Happiness, as the colonials and its Continental Congress had declared? Could not liberty for one be destitution for another; the definition could certainly vary, as was always the case in manifest destiny. And so, if a new nation were to arise, would it respect Aiegona and her borders and treaties or force her into a position of defending her preservation?

As much as he expected his homeland to triumph in any conflict with an emerging state out of Jhor's colonies, he remained perturbed by the reports of colonial reprisals to both loyalists and officers on the field; they were treated with malice and without mercy. It was perhaps one thing to ransack a home; houses could be rebuilt, but not souls: in the recent skirmish, published as the Battle of Clarkstown Bridge in colonial papers, the engagement was described to the horror of its readers, detailing the immoral acts and atrocities by His Majesty's regulars. Minutemen were made martyrs, but in reality they too committed barbarous acts, which revolutionary agitators simply decided to omit from print.

Hundreds lay dead following that skirmish, and much to the surprise of agitators (and relief of Aiegona as well as other neighboring states) but the colonies did not rise as one. Even with a publication declaring independence by its Continental Congress, the colonies remained fractured; although its representatives politicked and agreed to stake their lives and fortunes upon independence the commoner had his own life to safeguard, and few if any were so willing to set aside the tools of their trade to combat well-disciplined regulars in the field.

The Marquis did not blame them. What man in his right mind would dare face one of the most preeminent land armies in the world? Jhor was master of the sea and her armies were scaling defenses and capturing cities one after the next; she was a juggernaut. Even Aiegona trembled a bit at the diplomatic table, paying as much courtesy to her greatness as it could whenever negotiating a treaty or attempting to expand her own commercial prosperity. Jhor was unrivaled, but although she was defeating Romennal, she still had to contend with the influence and prominence of Bahn, a power whose colonial reach far outweighed her own. And in this game of majors and minors, the Marquis de Eliám knew his country's preservation depended on dancing a delicate waltz; pairing with the wrong partner or stepping out of rhythm could be disastrous.

And thus, as the colonial insurrection was poorly timed for Jhor in her war against Romennal, so too was it disconcerting for Aiegona, who not only feared her borders being invaded by an ambitious belligerent, but also a strain in the already tenuous relations that existed between her and Jhor; heavily influenced by Romennal, Aiegona prided herself on embracing Romennal customs, the latest fashion trends, and taking pleasure with good wine and song.

"If I may, you are quite young for an officer," the Marquis said, eager to converse with him. "I do not mean to be intrusive, but I hope we can share a few words before we arrive. I enjoy speaking to silence."

Leopaln smiled, happy to oblige. "I quite agree… on both accounts," he chuckled. "I was surprised myself to learn of my unusual orders this morning."

"Oh, pray tell," he said, judging the young man's character as he listened to Leopaln's journey. With relations strained as they were diplomatically with Jhor, the Marquis wondered if her officers were up to the task of containing the insurrection; a young man might run out of self-preservation in the heat of battle. So, would this young officer be one of them, he thought. If so, then surely these colonies could expect to become independent and Aiegona might need to mobilize her armies.

Perhaps more importantly than defending her borders and preserving trade with Jhor was continuing the profits earned by arms and munitions; war was profitable, and that fact was not lost on the Marquis, who was more than aware that his country sold to both Romennal and Jhor; a waltz of death whose choreography was left to diplomats and agents such as he: Jhor had protested with almost an air of arrogance, but at the charm and elegance of the Marquis both his government and the Parliament of Jhor had agreed to a satisfactory measure: the Marquis would make a tour of the colonies. In this way, his homeland might be assured of Jhor's capability to handle her domestic affairs, and if the Marquis's report were satisfactory then Aiegona would agree to embargo Romennal from arms and munitions.

The Nations: Fraternity

It was a suitable compromise, if nothing else simply a stratagem to buy time for both parties. Aiegona sought more profits, and Jhor needed time to transfer her invested armies. Moreover, it saved face between the two nations as well as with Romennal, who despite resenting Jhor might later be inclined to join in an alliance against the ever-growing influence of Bahn.

"So you are to command an entire company," said the Marquis, attracted to that fact. The young officer had perhaps confessed too much. "How do you feel about that?" To be honest, Leopaln was unsure. He had hardly expected it, but meant to do his best.

"I am an officer of Jhor, and I intend to do my duty," he said faithfully, to which the Marquis nodded at that. "I was assigned to these men," he added, "and I will perform my duties to the best of my abilities." He looked uncertain of how to do that, but brave enough to find a way. "I have been trained to lead men, and I shall do so even into battle if need be, seeking the help of my Guard Advice as often as I can."

The Guard Advice, the elite military voice of Jhor, was and had been for nearly a century advising her officers on tactics as well as day-to-day functions. Comprised of veterans with combat experience, they served as both a liaison between the rank and file and officer gentry as well as an additional line of communication within the chain of command: it was not

71

unusual for a Guard Advice attached to a general to discuss matters with another serving a colonel, particularly if timing was imperative; this exclusive right had proven time and again to be indispensible for quick, decisive action on the field, giving Jhor a formidable military advantage over her rivals:

Although she still followed conventional doctrines, Jhor espoused communication over maneuvers of position or movement, improving upon the traditional courier system such that any information high command might receive would have more validity behind it: a smaller network working alongside a larger network reaffirmed intelligence reports and subsequently enabled orders to move faster down the chain resulting in increased operational successes; neither Bahn nor Romennal had been able to emulate this martial innovation with much success, but then neither did they entirely consent to it, as one of its principle drawbacks was the tendency for arrogance. Being too heavily relied upon for their experience and efficacy gave the Guard Advice a sense of entitlement.

"Have you worked with any Guard Advice already?" the Marquis asked, suspecting the answer was no. It was no secret that green officers often depended too much on their Guard Advice instead of trusting their own judgment.

"I haven't, but I intend to take their word into consideration at the appropriate time."

The Marquis nodded. The young man's confidence in his decisions was assuring, and that was what Jhor needed now thought the Marquis, young men who could think for themselves instead of relying upon aged wisdom that while was experienced was perhaps not youthfully

"May I ask a personal question," he said, suddenly intrigued about the young man before him. The officer nodded. "Are you a faithful man, lieutenant?"

"How do you mean?"

"In faith there is loyalty," the Marquis said, questioning his own right to ask. He had religion, but was far from being a pious man; the loss of a wife and daughter did that for him. Nevertheless, he loved them and neither found solace in the arms of another woman nor forgot them, and in so doing he felt loyal to their memory. "When we believe in something so much that we are willing to hold onto it and fight for that, even die for that, we find ourselves steady in the face of life's adversities, and life will throw many our way. So, I ask, are you a faithful man in being who you are and standing by the virtues you believe in?"

Leopaln was astonished. He could hear the emotion in the man's voice, which resonated with past tragedy. He stumbled to answer at first so as not to offend. "I have faith in a higher power," he replied, "but my vigilance is first and foremost to myself. I believe God has enough to watch over that it's in my best interest to mind my own steps."

"Even if that takes you into fight you cannot win?" he asked, raising an eyebrow.

"I will do my duty, not for my sake, but for someone else."

"You have a love back home?"

"Yes sir, I do."

"Worth dying for?"

Leopaln swallowed hard. Death was hard enough to comprehend let alone being willing to accept; it was an uninvited guest to a party, who was neither easy to dismiss or ignore owing to its particular status. "I would die for her," he said, trying to believe in the words as he said them.

"Forgive me, but I am not convinced."

"I have been trained to lead not die, my lord. I am not convinced either that dying should be my first step on the battlefield; I will do all that I can before I walk through that door." The Marquis smiled. That was well said.

Leopaln turned his head to the window. The road along the woods had now opened into open countryside with scattered trees swaying in the growing breeze; the storm was nearing. He looked ahead to see the carriage was driving straight for it; as it winded a bend the driver smacked the reins harder and the horses galloped faster. There in the distance stood Fort Heritage, accentuating its prominence and fidelity as it rose above the landscape with a sharp prowess of her ramparts and sentries standing vigil. High above, her colors whipped in the wind and as the fort neared Leopaln could see regulars drilling, practicing formations and shifting patterns in rapid succession; on the grounds, he could also see the Guard Advice issuing drill orders and shouting over the wind.

As they approached the fort, he could see the cadenced drilling in more detail. Marching along the length of the walls to the command of the Guard Advice, the regulars rotated their formations in an array of patterns without defect, halting only to aim or practice advancing while aiming while the Guard Advice kept a vigilant watch over the discipline of each maneuver. Leopaln remembered the academy, but then thought of his friend. He hoped William would be all right.

As the carriage arrived, a sentry held up his hand and beckoned it to stop. "Afternoon to you, gentlemen," he said. "Please present your business to pass," he said. Leopaln handed him his orders. "But a minute sir, and we'll have the gate open for you." A moment later, the carriage passed through. It pulled up in front of small building under the shade of an oak tree; as the driver hopped down and opened the carriage door the commandant stepped out to greet them.

"Afternoon gentlemen," he said with a chuckle. "I expect you found Clarkstown pleasant enough. Come on in, and I expect one of you is my lieutenant," he joked. Inside was a sharp contrast from the other commandant's. Everything was in order and the man motioned with a steadiness of someone either prepared for the inevitable or already there; as they went into his office, his attendant handed him the quartermaster's report. "Place the order for additional supplies with Captain Rogers," he said, catching Leopaln's attention. The commandant didn't fail to notice that. "You know of that captain?"

"I do, sir. He is an old friend from the academy."

"A fine man and officer. He takes excellent care to make sure we are well provisioned; a bit fearful perhaps, but rest assure, gentlemen, this colonial matter is well under control. There won't be another incident."

The Marquis was less doubtful. "And may I ask what inspires this confidence," he said, introducing himself. Either the man was lying or overly confident of his resources.

The commandant smiled. "I have heard of you, sir, but please don't let gossip and rumors fill your head; it wasn't at all what the colonial papers would have you believe. Instead, it was just a scuffle with a few fatalities."

"I refer to your papers," snapped the Marquis, hardly in the mood for sweetening. "Now I will be blunt, commander. I

76

have spent the last few months at the behest of your government seeing for myself the condition of these colonies; and the facts do not lie, so please do not mistake me for some tourist." The commander tried to speak, but the man put his hand up. "I am not finished, and you will allow me to speak," he said firmly.

"I have had the pleasure of meeting with Captain Rogers, and the captain is anything but *a bit* fearful. He is a man stricken with grief, and it takes one to know one, but where I have had the time to weather my pain that man is overcome, and your supremacy in your irrationality is doing nothing to better his state of mind; I assure you commander, Clarkstown is as far from being amicable as any place I have ever been, and I have seen trepidation in my day, commander, and let me *assure* you that there was nothing that prepared me for the depravity and insurrection of that city; it is on the verge of revolution, if not there already."

For a moment there was silence. The commandant had tried but failed to disguise the truth, and now had the disrespect of his guest as well as the distrust. "My apologies," he said, finding no alternative but to ask forgiveness. "You are indeed correct, including the condition of the captain. I am the one who is fearful for him, as I fear for the future of these colonies;

we are in no position to hold our ground, and that's as blunt as I can be.

"I have enough men to deter insurrection here in the north, but the southern colonies are already lost; I have been in contact with the commandant down there and he assures me it is only a matter of time," he said, admitting the truth. "I am doing everything to preserve morale, but the reality is far from attractive; it will only take a catalyst to undo everything. My only hope is to delay the inevitable and if that means prolonging lies and falsehoods then so be it. I'd rather have my men confident, sober and ready then up all night waiting to die." He turned to Leopaln then. "I asked for a captain, but I have you instead," he said disappointed. "I hope you can handle your Guard Advice, because I can't transfer them. Frankly, nobody wants them," he said with disgust. "So congratulations, you just got the two most boorish Guard Advice in all of Jhor."

While the two continued conversing, Leopaln went out to meet them. After waiting ten minutes and then another five, he decided to find them; feeling awkward was almost as humiliating as waiting for someone who was supposed to be already waiting for you; they had neither come nor sent word of their tardiness. And so, he sought them out; the wind was picking up and the air was becoming chilly. High above, a hawk passed over the fort also in search, but for shelter.

Outside the parapets, he found them in dispute. Whereas one was taller than the other, the shorter, stockier of the two had a protruded, portly belly, and was quite animated: he pointed his finger and flung his arms in the air as if it helped compensate him for his smaller stature. The hefty of the two continued to elevate his voice, but his compatriot merely responded with short expressions, drawing more indignation from the other; back and forth they went, with seemingly no progress in their argument. Finally, the shorter one threw his arms up and stormed away. Leopaln headed in his direction to intercept.

"I am your new officer," he started to say, but the man just passed him by. Leopaln shouted after him, obliging him to turn about. "Well fancy that," the man said. "Now be a good lad and tell that tree behind you to mind his tongue."

Leopaln turned, uncertain to what the man meant, only to find the other Guard Advice was standing behind him. "Mr. Kepler, at your service, sir," the tall one said.

"More like keep up," the heftier one added.

"Don't mind him, sir," the other said, apologizing for his shorter companion's attitude. "He's just not tall enough to see sense."

"Why you half-witted turkey. I'll have you any day of the week you, just name it."

"How about last Friday, when I proved you wrong yet again," the man said, chuckling to his own dry humor. "Oh wait, I forgot. Sunlight can't reach under big rocks."

"Are you calling me daft?"

"That's funny," he said, throwing it back. "I didn't know rocks had names."

"Gentlemen, please," Leopaln said, interrupting them. "Now I have his name. Might I have yours also?" he asked.

"Mr. Henderson," the shorter one replied. He had a bald, round head with full cheeks. Beside him, his compatriot was indeed tall, towering at just over six feet; so tall in fact that his uniform was custom tailored. "And may I say it is a pleasure to meet you."

"Well, we were supposed to meet nearly thirty minutes ago," he said, pointing out their tardiness.

"Water under the bridge, sir," he said, dismissing it and trying to get in a jab. "Except for him, he can't fit." But Mr. Kepler was right there. "You find trolls under a bridge, sir," he said to Leopaln, passing the joke off as advice. "Best be careful with this one."

Leopaln couldn't help but lightly chuckle. So these were his Guard Advice, a couple of jokesters; the two stood facing him, neither looking at the other, but still exchanging wits.

"Tree."

"Rock."

"Well, anytime you're ready gentlemen," Leopaln said, trying to contain his laughter.

"Terribly sorry, sir," said Mr. Henderson. "Any chance we can move this indoors. It seems the weather has finally come about?"

"I concur."

"Well then, I'll fetch the rock cart," said Mr. Kepler, getting in the last bite.

Chapter 6

Discussing Many Matters

After listening to the orders, the Guard Advice concluded what Captain Rogers had postulated earlier, that the mission was to protect a convoy. Yet, of what baffled them altogether; surely munitions were worth the safeguard, but the double-edge of that was alerting rebel sympathizers. "Here's what bothers me," said Mr. Henderson, speaking freely, "there's no trouble there; there hasn't been since the skirmish a few months back. In fact, most of the agitation happening now is in the south. Besides, most folk living there are loyal to the crown and it's also regularly patrolled."

"Is it munitions," asked Mr. Kepler, also bemused. He rubbed his chin in bewilderment, but Leopaln shook his head. He had no idea. "Well, it's usually quiet there, but whatever it is we'll see it done. I'll assemble the company," he said, parting the room. As he left, Mr. Henderson continued his contemplation; he was not challenging the orders, merely trying to understand them. "There have been some reports of hostilities between a few landowners and the natives, but nothing too serious," he said, running his hand over his baldness. "Still, what sort of convoy would require an entire company to escort it, certainly not commercial? So, if it isn't that or munitions, then what is it?"

Leopaln offered a thought. "Perhaps it's not something, but someone," he said, thinking about the foreign dignitary he had traveled with. "If it were someone of importance, perhaps that might warrant such protection."

The Guard Advice considered it, but then shook his head. If he were on horseback then perhaps, but this man would no doubt be traveling by carriage; an armed escort on foot would only slow his journey. "It is not that I question the order, sir," he said, taking an abrupt pause. "It is that ambiguity can result in heavy losses, and I do not wish to repeat history if it can be avoided."

"What do you mean?"

"Six hundred spirited lads marched up that hill," he said, recalling the skirmish a few months back. "The rebels had taken up a position on the Mound of the Miller, entrenched behind a barricade of fallen timbers. Our orders were simple enough, dislodge and scatter. And while we advanced in good form, fife and drum to our pace, awaiting the volley of those

83

undisciplined farmers, it became all too clear that something was amiss; what we expected was not what was waiting for us.

"To think of these colonials as farmers with a pitchfork is to commit a grave sin, sir. They are resourceful, determined and resolved; and they had rolled up a cannon. It was only as we neared did I realize what we were really up against. These are passionate men, willing to die for what they believe in; and the last time I had seen that was in the face of a Romennal boy I killed." His voice dropped.

"Probably no more than sixteen, but did he ever have heart. It was as if he already knew his fate, because we locked eyes and I could see it in him, that look of admission; he knew as I did that he stood no chance, but he raised his weapon anyway. I shot that boy, not because I could or was better trained, but because I was afraid, because he was braver than I. And that's how these colonials are, resolved and unyielding."

"Is that why you're here instead of Romennal?"

He nodded. "I am a man, just a man, and until the day I die I will never be able to forget that boy's face; not even an ocean can separate me from that fact. And mind you this sir, the colonials that we faced that day were men and boys, and once again I came face to face with a lad, only this time I couldn't pull the trigger."

"So he lived to fight another day?"

"No, somebody else shot him," he said, vacantly. "I follow my orders, but I have no desire to face my nightmares again without being ready," he added. "If it's indeed a convoy then so be it; if it is something else entirely, then I wish to be prepared. I'm not afraid of dying or killing, but I'd rather not face my demons without a rehearsal in my mind of what to expect."

"And what about Mr. Kepler? Is he also of the same conviction?"

The Guard Advice chuckled. "You can ask the giant yourself," he said as Mr. Kepler stepped back into the room.

"To whom are you calling a giant, troll-man?" he snickered. "When you're ready sir, the men are formed, but owing to the weather I urge we leave tomorrow."

"Thank you Mr. Kepler, and we shall, but I first wish to inspect the men."

From a distance, the Marquis watched with keen interest as the young officer inspected his men; something bemused him. Was it his rank? Surely, a captain was better suited for leading so many, or was it the youth's confidence? Nevertheless, he seemed quite adept at leading; the academy of Jhor was well renowned, but the Marquis was unsure if Leopaln was simply hiding his fear or if he was simply a good actor, staging a strong performance. "Then again," Nate said, reading his master's thoughts, "Some men simply rise to the occasion."

The Marquis chuckled. "Indeed, some men do."

Of all men, Nate and he knew best. Both had endured unbearable hardship, and though his companion had met the lashings of a whip the Marquis succumbed to intense but brief sessions of grief on occasion; he refused the company of others, even barred the light from his room with heavy drapes, refusing to be seen in such a deplorable state. He had loved them and still did, and while he tried to channel the pain towards productive activities each and every day it still grieved him nevertheless.

He relied upon Nate, not just for his companionship, but because he understood his anguish; as tranquil and serene as nature as it was still not enough to restrain his suffering. The lush forests of Aiegona, its rivers, hilly countryside and even the chirping of birds were not enough to silence the tormenting screams of that night. He had to watch them die, and he was helpless to do anything about it.

"I think I'd like to take a walk," he said solemnly to Nate, who joined him in silence; whenever the Marquis needed to think he walked. "I find that the prowess of a nation isn't so much about how many soldiers she has, but the quality of its citizens," he said. "I have lived long enough to say with absolute conviction that a soldier should be a citizen first, because it is the barber and the schoolteacher who will restrain from punishing the innocent when they have been conquered; and therein lies a fundamental quality of any nation, that its people, not its policies, establish its reputation among nations.

"You speak of Jhor?"

"I do, for in her martial and economic dexterity she promotes the values, morals and principles that give her navies and armies a strength unparalleled; when free men are given a chance to discover love and hardship on their own then they give back more to the state, and this is often taken for granted. We forget that freedom is born from the womb of oppression and that in many places in the world education is suppressed, that tribal warlords and barons afar keep their people ignorant, and that an educated man can become more prosperous than his despotic neighbor.

"But it is in that freedom that we also forget to remind ourselves of where we came from, and that is where I believe Jhor now stands; she has forgotten her past, she has forgotten the hardship that brought about her prosperity, and I see in that young man both a perpetuation of mistakes as well as the possibility of hope."

"How so," Nate asked.

"The value of being young is bringing about change."

Chapter 7

What Mr. Harmlukc Spoke of

The company drilled for the greater part of the morning and as they prepared to march out Leopaln received a rider from Clarkstown. The man retrieved a letter from his haversack; it was a letter from William, requesting his presence.

Leopaln, my dear old friend,

How benevolent you are! Please forgive my earlier leave of senses, for it is not the William you knew, and would not wish for you to remember me as such if these are too be shorter days for us. I beckon you to forgive my misconduct, and join me briefly in Clarkstown. I shall not keep you long, but I had of late forgotten the joy of friendship and would truly be honored by your acceptance. I ask this of you to amend my wrongs and secure the friendship we have held for so long.

Yours truly,

Capt. William Rogers

Leopaln thanked the rider and secured permission from the commandant, who felt helpless to refuse. "How can I deny the man who supplies us," he said admittedly, "especially a man in his state! If he is your friend, then do whatever you can to bring him back."

But William was perhaps too far-gone, for back in Clarkstown Leopaln saw the full extent of his friend's malady. His attendants had all but given up trying to maintain the décor; everywhere furnishings were destroyed and paintings lay on the floor, forced from their hangings by rage and disease, and William stood staring up at the corner in the ceiling. "Ah, Leopaln, there you are. Wonderful to see you," he said happily, as if nothing was out of place. "Shall we?"

Outside, the fresh air did the captain some good and he swelled his lungs with it. "A fine day," he said cheerfully, taking each stride with pleasure. "Please forgive my conduct yesterday. I was not myself."

"It seems that continues to be the case," Leopaln said, hinting at the sight he just saw. "You are sick William, and you need help."

The captain smiled assuredly. "I am quite fine, truly I am. I just had a bad day yesterday, nothing more."

"And how many bad days do you usually have?"

"Perhaps that's true," he admitted, "but let us not be bothered by that now. You are here and that is all that matters to me."

"As you wish. And so where are we headed?"

"For good food and company," William said with a grateful smile. With Leopaln he was at peace, parlaying a truce with the demons inside, for had his friend arrived an hour earlier he would have seen him in full anguish; he had sliced one painting in half with his sword and fired his pistol into a sofa, cursing every last colonial that breathed air.

But now he smiled trying to forget the torment, and instead looking ahead. He had thrown books and ledgers across the room, shattered mirrors and smashed a chair; the pain in his head was unbearable and was only alleviated by his friend's presence. "I do miss those days at the academy," he said, jovially, remembering good times.

As he shared old memories, Leopaln was pleased to see his spirits rise. His friend was more chipper now, returning to his old self, laughing and telling stories with a contagious exuberance; as the two of them walked and talked, they forgot about the war, the colonial rebellion, and all matters except the good times they had. "I recall you struggled in mathematics and languages," he chuckled. "So, how on earth did you become an officer without your father's help?"

"Whatever do you mean?" he said, trying to skirt the topic. "I exceled in geometry. It was you that failed your trigonometry exam."

"Which is why I'm not in the royal artillery!"

"That's probably a good thing."

"Now whatever do you mean by that," he said, pretending to take offense.

Leopaln raised an eyebrow. "Well, by the looks of your office you hit pretty much everything."

"That's not funny."

"Yes, it is, admit it," he chuckled.

"Alright, yes, I see your point."

"Are we close yet to where we're going?"

"Actually, here it is," said William, stopping beside a tavern where an old man sat outside, reading the newspaper and smoking his pipe. "Mr. Harmluck," he called out, but the man ignored him. So, he called out again.

"I heard you the first time, captain," he said with a snicker, "I just decided life is better when you hear your name called out twice."

"And why is that?"

"Because it's more fun that way," he chuckled. "Come on over lads and take a seat." As they sat, commoners passed by, talking, gossiping and keeping to their business.

"Who is your friend?" he asked the captain.

"His name is Leopaln, and he is very old friend of mine," William replied happily.

"Well, any friend of the captain's is a friend of mine, and to what do I owe the pleasure of this visit? As you can tell, I'm a very busy man these days," he jested.

"I can tell, but maybe you could fit in a tale or two."

"A tale you say?" he said. "Fancy that. I happen to be in a rather likeable mood for that."

The elderly man was unshaven, but otherwise his appearance was dignified. He had thick brows and a full set of hair covered by a three-cornered cap. "But how can I begin a tale without meat and drink?" He called over a waiter and ordered for the table. "A round for the table and bring me enough to last," he said, and then turning to the captain. "I expect my tale won't have a tail," he said, handing him the bill.

William smiled, almost embarrassingly. "But of course not," he said. Mr. Harmluck refused to believe in a free lunch, unless he was eating, but even then he was the owner of the establishment and despite the captain being a regular customer his coin was expected; after all, business was business and the captain's gold was worth far more than the worthless colonial paper. "Every man has to eat," said the old philosopher.

"True, but are you giving me a fish or just teaching me to fish?" replied the captain.

Mr. Harmluck was quick on his wit. "Why teach you? I'll be out of business. And now," he said, turning to Leopaln, "would you care for a story as the captain has requested?"

"That sounds fine by me."

"Very well," he said, looking at the two of them. "I think I know just the tale to tell. It begins with friends, much like the two of you. Our story takes place a long time ago, before Jhor ruled the seas, before the colonies, and even before this so-called new world was discovered. Our story begins in a land far to the south called Bladaria. He noticed Leopaln's ears perk up. "So you've heard of this land?"

"Only in a story my father used to tell me as a boy."

"Then you'll recognize much of what I say, but perhaps the lesson behind it will be different," he said going on. "Indeed, the skirmish here recently is nothing compared to what happened centuries ago in this part of the world. Today, Bladaria doesn't exist, and for good reason; the only vision that came out of that land was ruin.

"But I'm getting ahead of myself; so let me start from the beginning. Nearly three centuries ago, a great man united his people, declared a nation reborn, and then carried his vision into other lands that did not take lightly to it; now remember that

Bladaria existed in the southwest of this continent, but is now occupied by its neighbor, Lameria, and she is a colossus, giving apprehension to any warmonger. Today, she is strong, governed by a rich aristocracy, but in the days of our story she was divided, weak, and ripe for the plundering.

"Now this great man was named Goshen, as you might know," he said gesturing to Leopaln. "Now Goshen went by many names, Goshen the Great, Goshen the Visionary, or to the Lamerians, Goshen the Vanquisher. He was a behemoth of a man and it is said that the earth opened up and gave him birth and he returned that debt by putting thousands back into it."

Mr. Harmluck changed his tobacco. "Now Goshen was no more a man than you or I, but he had uncanny charisma and that drew men to him like hens to feed. As it was, Bladaria in those days was ravaged by war and plague, and men squabbled for power, filling graves and pocketing as much gold as they could while hunger wiped families off the map; not exactly what I'd call pleasant times, but out of this came Goshen, and he brought the nobles together with his vision.

"Now as I said, he was a man of charisma and he had a way of pulling people towards him, but bear in mind he was not of noble blood, and that didn't sit well with the nobles, who conspired against him, but that's getting ahead of ourselves. Goshen was a commoner and the people loved him; his vision of a united land grabbed folk everywhere and made them an unconquerable force; the nobles had no choice but to go along.

"Now then, this brings us to the point of my tale. Goshen had a brother, and the two were as close as any brothers could be, but he did not believe in his vision; he did believe in a united land, but one free of the nobles. After all he argued, what's the difference between a united land under oppression and or a divided land that was still corrupt; Goshen would not listen though, and instead demanded his brother believe in his visionary leadership; as the rift widened between these two brothers so the nobles took advantage of that." The food arrived and Mr. Harmluck continued while the officers ate.

"Now Bladaria is a very ancient land, and its traditions and politics are as old as its forests; what Goshen wanted was a united land, but his brother wanted something more, a free land. But freedom wasn't what Goshen wanted. He wanted adoration, to be worshipped as if proclaiming himself a deity; it filled his head and corrupted him. The more that followed him the more he believed he was a blessing to Bladaria. And surely as day becomes night, the two brothers tore apart from one another, going their separate ways.

"Now Goshen united the land, not by the sword but by his vision. That isn't to say there wasn't any bloodshed; certainly many disagreed and Goshen made an example out of them, but he declared them to be non-believers and burned their flesh for all to see; it is said the burning of one nobleman was attended by others, who watched and did nothing as the commoner Goshen denounced the man to be a heretic; the fact that not one nobleman interrupted Goshen and had him arrested, or even had him burned alive, tells us that whether people believed in his vision or not they were unwilling to go against him. He had gathered too many followers, and martyring him would only have aroused the populace against the nobles; better to make a deal with the devil than to be cast into purgatory."

"And what became of his brother," William asked. He did not know the tale as well as the other two.

Mr. Harmluck stared at the two of them for a moment. "You're good lads, and I like you both. Perhaps it is best to leave the story as it is."

"Surely you cannot," said the captain, jesting. "I must hear the end. Please, I implore you."

"Aye, very well, but remember you asked to hear it. Well, Goshen united the land and celebrated his triumph with a wedding, taking a bride of noble blood and proclaiming himself king; with the people on his side, the nobles had no choice but to yield; but that's not to say they didn't try and prevent it. After all, a king was of noble blood. So, how could he wear the crown legally? These noblemen were sly and crafty, hosting banquets in his honor but sharpening their blades behind his back. They thanked him for his direction, urging him to retire in wealth and dignity, exclaiming that he had given so much to his land and people that he deserved a rest, but Goshen incensed them by refusing.

"Instead, he not only enlarged his vision but also declared himself to be an exception to the laws and customs of the land, stating that although he was born a commoner he was obviously a natural leader and thus entitled to all the statuses and privileges that he so desired. As the people cheered at his coronation the nobles readied their armor; they had loathed Goshen's brother, but now sought him out. After all, the enemy of my enemy is my friend."

The captain sat back in disbelief. "Brother against brother. Oh my. Mr. Harmluck, you surely know how to tell a story!"

The man winked, "I surely try, captain. Now as I was saying, the nobles came before the brother and offered an alliance. Blood may be thicker than water, but Goshen had to be stopped. He was no longer humble; fame and fortune had gone to his head and to make matters worse he had declared war on Lameria, embracing his new vision of a united land under him; if you think the people wavered you're wrong. They cheered for their savior and marched with him, crushing aside the armies of

Lameria; as I said, Lameria was weak, but she did have resolve and despite being conquered she fought bitterly for every inch. Goshen was now master of all he surveyed and he had only to enlarge his vision and the people followed him. He was a bold visionary to many, a conqueror, and a hero, and it seemed as if he was untouchable.

"But when he tried to take a second wife his brother finally intervened. She was a noblewoman of Lameria and he justified the marriage that it united both lands and that the seed of the union would bring peace and prosperity; as the legend goes, the people hesitated but consented, still believing in him and his vision. But what he did next opened their eyes. The brother interrupted the ceremony and denounced it as treason. He demanded his brother return to Bladaria and give up his vision, but Goshen was filled with zeal, as it is said, he killed his own kin. Then he turned around and demanded the ceremony continue."

"Wait, what? He did not even mourn his brother?"

"Why should he?" Mr. Harmluck said, playing his role as storyteller. "To him, his brother was a non-believer."

"Surely, but that is one's kin. I cannot believe he would so heartlessly leave the corpse of his brother on the floor and demand the wedding to continue."

"But that is what the tale says happened."

"Truly, I have not heard such a thing in all my life," the captain marveled. "If Leopaln were injured I would come to his rescue, as I know he would do likewise."

"And I have no doubt he would," the old man said, believing him. "No doubt at all."

Chapter 8

A Change in Orders

As the three enjoyed their meal, a dispatch came riding hurriedly down the street. "Sir, this just arrived from the commandant in South Anchorage Point," he said, dismounting before them.

"Is it urgent?" asked Mr. Harmluck, curiously. "And will I be finishing this meal alone?"

"I'm afraid you may," William apologized, reading the dispatch. "Leopaln, we must be off."

"Then to the next time," the old man toasted, raising his glass, "and to the pleasure of fine company."

"Of friends, Mr. Harmluck?" William jested, knowing the old man too well.

"Well, you can have friends and I'll have women."

"But which is finer company?"

The old man smiled. "I'd say you take yours and I'll take mine and will let happiness   decide."

The Nations: Fraternity

He chuckled. "Fair enough," he said, tipping his hat and wishing him a good rest of his day. As the two officers departed, Mr. Harmluck nursed his drink and stoked his pipe, pondering what matter of urgency had stolen his friends away; he liked the captain, and wished him all the best of health, but he knew the man suffered.

Hardship was nothing new for the colonies, or those coming to it. It was a cornerstone in its foundation, and those who stayed long enough became accustomed to its adversity; those migrating westward provoked the natives, and those in verbal defiance to the Crown suffered as much as those that drew arms against it. And though Mr. Harmluck spoke his opinion, unconcerned of the consequences at his age, he nevertheless condemned both sides, alleging that only through hardship could both see the contradictions in their arguments: the Continental Congress, representing all the colonies, had declared independence but neither was prepared for it nor could accomplish much through voting. And yet, His Majesty and Parliament were no better, involving Jhor and her colonies into a protracted war with Romennal that only now seemed to be concluding, and for what, gold, glory and prestige? He sneered. Old men bickered while young men died, and in the process the financial burden had incensed her colonies, which felt they were paying a greater share of it.

No taxation without representation, agitators had cried aloud, demanding a stronger voice in Parliament to argue the merits of taxing colonial citizens more heavily than others. It was unjust, but then hardship was part of the colonies, whether given or received, and if Jhor needed to learn that then so be it; she may have the mightiest force on earth, but it meant nothing to a son born in the colonies who was bred of struggle.

"Your orders are being changed," said William irate, as he and Leopaln hurried off. "It seems the rebels have been busy, and there's nothing to prevent that." He handed it to him, who hastily read it. Suddenly and without warning, William stopped and laughed. "Finer company, oh Mr. Harmluck."

"What is funny?" he asked bemused, taken aback by his friend's change in demeanor. Apparently there was a joke he had missed.

"Mr. Harmluck was jesting. I didn't catch it until just now."

"I don't follow?"

"He said, to the pleasure of fine company. He was referring to us, to officers. It's a joke here in the colonies." Leopaln still didn't understand. "It means an officer's company is better than anyone else's, because an officer will toast for you while a beggar will do nothing but appeal to your heart, a merchant to your purse, and a soldier to your spirit; all of which of these do nothing but distract you."

"Finer company for a meal," said Leopaln, now understanding better. "That does seem true, I suppose. But what of these orders," he asked, getting back to the urgency at hand. "What of the supposed convoy that my company is to protect."

"I don't think there was ever a convoy."

"But what else could it have been?"

"Truthfully, I think it was your father," he said, a bit agitated that Leopaln was still refusing to believe in that possibility. "I think he assigned you a company not to protect something, but someone and that person was you." Leopaln started to speak, but William cut him off. "You keep denying it, but that's the reality of it. You're not just some officer, you are your father's son, and not even my father has that much pull. Accept it, Leopaln, because whether you like him or not, he's still your father and he's still looking out for you, even if there's an ocean separating the two of you."

Leopaln tried to ignore him. It wasn't true, he refused to believe it was so, but William grabbed him by the coat. "The truth hurts, alright, I know, but you are my friend Leopaln, and I would never do anything to intentionally hurt you. I just want you to accept what is reality."

Leopaln shot him a glare. In his heart, he wanted to believe him, but his hatred refused to. "Even if it was true, I still would not believe it."

"But why?"

"Because I hate him, that's why! He's a monster."

"He's your father!"

"Don't William. Just don't."

"The truth hurts, but it's what we learn by and we learn best from experience, which is nothing more than truth shoved in our face. So, I don't care if you hate me too, but what other explanation is there?"

Leopaln turned away from him. Two thousand miles away and his father was still dictating terms to him, directing his life the way he saw fit; he cursed the man, and wished he had never been born, better to die than be that man's son. All he could think of was their last argument, how his father had still refused to recognize him and his wishes and even accused his one true love of being a burglar.

His eyes wandered, and all he saw before him was depravity, a city filled with people mocking him and what he stood for; he cursed them too. He cursed ever-setting foot in the colonies, and now regretted even accepting William's offer. He should have just left with the company and ignored any dispatch to order him back; but could he defy his friend as well as his father?

"I know you mean well, William, but please don't speak any more of this. As much as I believe you, I don't wish to; I want to hate him, so can't you let me have that?" He thought of back home. He thought of her, and the yellow cloth he had bought her. All he wanted was the sensual warmth of her body against his; he missed her and longed to look into her eyes once more.

"I am your friend, Leopaln, always and forever."

"Then let me have this."

"And what of me? What do I get in return?" he asked, sensing the demons scratch harder inside of him. "What can you give me that will cure me?"

"I have nothing," he offered. "I can only promise that our friendship will never end."

William smiled faintly. "That's good enough for me."

As Leopaln hurried back to Fort Heritage, the sky darkened once again, only at a faster pace this time and rain began to pour; even before it was in sight, the driver was soaked. Leopaln glanced out the window, but could see nothing except a trail of water scampering across the glass. He thought about what William had said, and though it pained him he believed him; if anyone knew his father it was he. The two were as close as any friends could be, and as much as it pained him to see William suffer, so it must have pained him to see Leopaln lie to himself.

As the carriage came over a hill, the driver smacked the reins harder and looked to his lantern, hoping it would be seen. Over the road the carriage tore without sight of Fort Heritage and to the driver's fortune a sentry noticed him. All at once, there was a hastening to open the gate, but against the mud the door refused to budge; in full dash more soldiers rushed over to help, cursing and struggling as they put their backs into it.

They pulled at the gate with great heaves, but the only stirring came from the perspiring and elevating tempers as feet slid in the mud; Mr. Henderson and Mr. Kepler joined in and screeched curses against the wretched mud that defied their every attempt; as the downpour hastened their strength depleted, but neither the Guard Advice nor their regulars were willing to surrender. Stubborn to the very end, Mr. Henderson issued shouts to the men to put their backs into it; they were exhausted but did as they were told, and against the weight of mud and rain the gate finally opened just as the carriage came tearing in.

Chapter 9

The Debacle of South Anchorage Point

Neither the Marquis nor the commandant were pleased by the news of the letter, the former for its ominous tone, perturbing everyone in the room, and the latter simply because the last person he wished to be in the room was there; if the situation was shaky at best before now it was far much worse. "And may I ask why?" said the Marquis de Eliám, wishing to understand the gravity of the letter better. "Because as I look about this room, even your attendants seem disconcerted by this letter."

The commandant excused everyone, except the foreigner and Leopaln. Against his better judgment he decided to explain what was happening. "If the lieutenant isn't aware already," he said uneasily, "South Anchorage Point is a port-city in the south; it is what Clarkstown is in the north, except for perhaps one major difference. It doesn't have much of a garrison, not to say we have much, but the commandant there has even less to work with; every day that passes is a blessing for those men there as well as one for us too. I have orders to protect Clarkstown and to the best of my ability I believe I have done that, but whereas the few hundreds I have can just barely dissuade rebel sympathies that hope is nonexistent in the south; to wit, there is nothing to save South Anchorage Point should the rebels attack it."

"And will they?" asked the Marquis, suspecting the inevitable. "For it seems they would."

"More than likely, as an outlet to the sea would offer promises of foreign aid, especially from our enemies."

"Such as Romennal?"

"To say the least," he sneered. "If I were them I'd be seizing every opportunity to exploit the weak chinks in our armor."

"And so what do you make of this letter that comes with such haste? Is haste to be its reply as well, and should then the lieutenant be assembling *his* company of men to march south then?" he said with a subtle wink of friendliness. The Marquis had a good feeling about him, and if Leopaln would not seize upon providence then he would do so for him. "I believe the lieutenant is more than capable of seeing this through," he said, toasting his talents. "He is young, steadfast, and I had the pleasure of getting to know him on the way here originally. I would say it is highly unlikely Jhor would find herself such another as he for some time."

The commandant clasped his hands behind his back, apprehensive about sending an unseasoned officer on such an errand; as able as he may well be the lieutenant appeared more a boy than a man. To risk an entire company, nearly one-third of the garrison on such an expedition required someone of more experience. "As promising as that may be I am not in favor of the idea."

"And pray tell why is that?"

"I have other officers who are more experienced."

"True," replied the Marquis, giving his support to Leopaln. It was as unexpected as it was surprising. "But youth and imagination are not hindered by experience; a seasoned officer is cautious, conservative, predictable."

"These aren't soldiers," he corrected him. "They're just colonials."

"Who happen to have excellent marksmanship," he added, raising his brow to that critical point. "Hardly peasants with pitchforks. Wouldn't you agree?" he said, arousing the man's antipathy; it was as resentful as it was provoking, and if the Marquis were any other man the commandant would have excused him from the room.

"I decide the orders of my men," he said, irate.

A. Ruben

But the Marquis was resolute. "Then perhaps you would care to explain to your superiors how your decision cost a valuable asset; if I am not mistaken, the lieutenant's men are mobilized and ready to march out. Any further delays will only increase the chances of losing the city."

"You overstep yourself sir," he replied. "You are a guest, not an advisor."

"Perhaps, but the fact remains that your superiors will submit to the politics of your statesmen, who sent me here."

The commandant stared at him indignantly. With one leg crossed over the other and his head perched against his hand he tapped his cheek bitterly, thinking about how much he despised politics getting involved in military affairs. The Marquis had him cornered, but for what purpose escaped him; to what end did he want Leopaln to go instead of a more seasoned officer? After all, wouldn't that be more pleasing to report on? There were too many questions and not enough answers, and the clock in the corner struck the hour. He did not agree, but it seemed he had little choice. "If this is the will of His Majesty's neighbors, then so be it. I have no interest in the politics."

The Marquis nodded, appreciating his understanding. "Then may I offer a toast?"

"A toast for what?"

"To the health of Jhor and her colonies of course," he replied, pouring the three of them a glass. The commandant however was still feeling a bit insulted.

"To Jhor, His Majesty and Parliament."

"To neighbors at peace."

"To a new world order of peace," he said, throwing it back as he raised his glass. "May the high seas always know the flag of Jhor."

The Marquis stepped closer to him, narrowing his glare. He raised his glass and the two men drank distrustful of one another. "May it all rest in the hands of this young man."

In the moonlight, the Marquis silently boarded his carriage. He had expected to leave in the morning, but changed plans at the last minute. "I am weary, Nate," he said, resting his head. "If you need me I shall be dreaming of better times."

"A long evening," his manservant said with a smile.

"An exhaustive one. Jhor is without a doubt the most abrasive neighbor we have ever had."

"How so?"

"She doesn't recognize potential, even when it's right in front of her."

"God help us all."

"Indeed, God help us."

"To where are we headed then, sir?" he asked.

The Marquis closed his eyes. "South, Nate. Let's see what's happening there."

Chapter 10

What Happened on the March South

The company began its march at first light, but a downpour quickly deluged the road, slowing their pace considerably. At night, they quartered in villages and rose early to make up for lost time; the Guard Advice did their best to keep morale high, but another rainstorm withered their spirits. "Curse this rain," Mr. Henderson said, tired of it already.

"I don't know. It helps shine your head," his compatriot said, trying to be uplifting. Mr. Henderson burst out laughing with the lads joining. Even Leopaln couldn't help but smile; the humor of his Guard Advice was pleasing at times.

"The two of you never cease to humor them," he said, noting how the company seemed to have a personal liking to Mr. Henderson and Mr. Kepler.

"It's the pleasure of our company," Mr. Henderson replied lightly. "You see some Guard Advice are strict, demanding much of their men, but old tree and I put it on the lads. We believe in high standards, push them and they'll rise to the occasion; it's all about accountability, and as much as we expect of them we push ourselves even more. You'll see soon enough, in the thick of battle these lads won't let you down."

Mr. Kepler nodded. "They're well trained by us," he added. "They'll make you proud."

"Were they engaged with the rebels earlier?"

"Aye that they did. And best believe it when I say that they owed that victory to their discipline than by any Guard Advice there including Mr. Kepler or myself."

"You are very proud of them then?"

"To the living and the fallen, sir. These lads are good men and will see it done, whatever command you give."

Leopaln smiled faintly at that respect, but something still bemused him, something the commandant had said. "I was told that transferring you and Mr. Kepler is rather difficult, that no other command wants you. Is that true?"

A stern look spread across the man's face, as if the issue were touchy. "Aye, that's true, but not because of any poor quality of either of us; rather it is because of something you will soon encounter: the problem isn't who has the better advice, the Guard Advice or the officers, but rather who is willing to listening and learn." Mr. Kepler nodded in agreement. "You see,

I've advised many officers in the past, but either he feigns listening and does his own thing or he listens too much and neglects his own duties, opting to put all accountability on us, including failure.

"Lord Horwick, who I expect you've heard about his triumphs in the newspapers, is the former. His Guard Advice are well acquainted with Mr. Kepler and I, and as such we know that his lordship is as much revered as he is loathed, particularly for his iron will disposition; he will listen, but rarely does he act on the guidance of his Guard Advice."

The company came to a fork in the road and the company halted. "Rest here lads," Mr. Henderson said. Out of habit he had issued orders, which Leopaln felt uneasy about, but permitted. "It's not that I meant any disrespect," the man said, "just old habits."

"The last commanding officer permitted it?"

"He did, but then that's what saved his life a number of times up until the end," he said, thinking fondly of him. "He was a good man."

"How did he die?"

"A rebel got a lucky shot."

"I hear these are more than just farmers with pitchforks, so I seriously doubt it was a lucky shot."

The Guard Advice faintly smiled. "I suppose that's half true, but remember in the thicket of it everything comes down to discipline. These colonials are excellent shots, but they require more time to be accurate in their aim. So, like I said, it was a lucky shot."

Leopaln stared off, thinking if that would be his fate too. The countryside was serene and tranquil, offering a bit of peace to a restless mind. "I believe we go left," he said, retrieving a map from his coat pocket.

"We'll take both roads," said Mr. Kepler, joining them. He had gone down the line to inspect everyone was in good order and nothing was out of place.

That puzzled Leopaln. "How so?" he asked.

"We'll make better time that way, and besides these two roads run parallel to each other. So, we won't be too far from either column. Mr. Henderson agreed. It was a wise course of action. "But it's your call, sir."

As Mr. Kepler led one to the right, Leopaln and Mr. Henderson took the other left, and as some of the lads picked up a tune Leopaln again inquired about the habits of his Guard Advice. "I smoke only fine southern tobacco," the man said, jesting.

"Do do you expect we will overcome this?" he asked.

"What this rebellion? Most certainly, well at least I will. You on the other hand, well that's between you and God."

"Are you a religious man, Mr. Henderson?"

"Let's just say I have my moments of faith," he replied. "Being in the army all my life has given me a certain perspective on life and death. I've seen good lads perish and many more survive; to me, it's all a lottery."

"An interesting way of looking at it," mused Leopaln.

"Well, not when I should have taken up a tontine," he laughed. "I'm still kicking hard."

"How many of them do you believe will survive?"

"A bit morbid don't you think, but perhaps still a fair question," he said, curious as to the officer's somber tone. "I reckon most will, but again that's largely owed to their discipline and whether they follow their training."

"Do you expect we will find any trouble this way?"

The Guard Advice thought for a moment. "This way takes us south along the Merchant Road, which has had some occasional native reports, and I suspect that's why Mr. Kepler insisted on dividing our forces; while that runs the risk of either column endangering itself, it's still better than an entire column falling into an ambush."

"And how long before we reach the border?" he asked, examining the map.

117

"Three weeks."

"That'll certainly stretch our provisions, so where do you suggest we stop and resupply?

Mr. Henderson pointed to places on the map. "There are plenty of towns and villages along the Merchant Road, but I'm not sure which are sympathetic to the rebels. We may just have to take our chances. But that's not really our problem."

Leopaln shot him a look of puzzlement. "Well then, what is?"

He pointed to a stretch along the Merchant Road. "It narrows here with dense woodlands on either side. If we are to expect trouble it will be there."

"Then we must alert Mr. Kepler at once!"

"Again, why do you think he insisted?" he said with a smirk. "I trust that man more than I do my own moral compass," he said, taking out his flask and having a sip. "I promised him I would stop years ago. Guess I'm no saint."

Leopaln was still uneasy about the idea though. The thought of walking into a possible ambush was unsettling. "Are you saying we may be walking into trouble?"

"No, what I'm saying is that that man knows what he's doing, and even I know when to listen to that old tree." But as night descended Leopaln became even more apprehensive, ordering the company to suddenly halt before it reached the thicket.

"What do you think you're doing?" Mr. Henderson snapped at him unexpectedly.

"Avoiding unnecessary risks. We will proceed ahead in the morning."

"No we will continue ahead as planned."

"You forget yourself, Mr. Henderson."

"I certainly have if you've lost your senses, sir. Mr. Kepler is out there with half of the column, or do you intend to abandon them?"

A trickle of rain began to pour. "I intend to keep as many lives out of unnecessary harm as possible."

"We're in the colonies. There's no such thing!"

"You will quiet yourself, Mr. Henderson," but the man's belligerence only elevated.

"I have served a lot longer than you. I know more things and have seen far more than you can possibly begin to imagine! Now this company marches or as God as my witness I will have you placed in irons for failing to execute and endangering the lives of others with your cowardice."

Leopaln was taken aback. He had never expected to hear such words from his Guard Advice nor in the least in front of the column, which were now suddenly raising doubts about his leadership; they were accustomed to Mr. Henderson more so than him. His obstinacy to authority and high standard of discipline was no secret, but the lieutenant was new. They didn't know much about him, except that he was remarkably young for his command, and now as the rain began to pour harder they stood quietly awaiting orders.

"This column marches," Mr. Henderson said definitively, preparing to issue the order. Leopaln ordered him to cease, but the Guard Advice ignored him.

"You intend to march them into death!" he said over the rain, trying to curry favor with the column that suddenly exchanged looks of concern. "If we continue down this road we may find death."

"Aye, and I hope we do, because I'll show its arse to the door and so will these lads. You fear death, stay behind. Forward, march!"

"Company halt."

"Don't," Mr. Henderson threatened. "Don't come between me and this column. You can stand in the front and take all the glory when we win, but these lads belong to me. I am their keeper and I will do whatever it takes to preserve them, and right now I'm about to lose half of them, so get out of my way boy."

Any other officer may have challenged their Guard Advice right then and there, ordering him placed into irons for insubordination and disrespect of an officer, but something in the man's voice seemed genuine and urgent, as if he knew something that Leopaln did not. "You said there was only a possibility of something, but I don't believe you. I think you know something. Are we in danger?"

The Guard Advice stared at him, deciding whether to continue his berating or tell him; he didn't an eye in the back of his head to know the column was wondering too. "There is a report of natives in the area. They rarely come this far to the east, but with the colonies in rebellion it has strengthen their resolve."

Leopaln stepped closer to him, ignoring the rain and forgetting about the argument they just had. "How many?"

"Not enough for Mr. Kepler to handle on his own."

As the company hurriedly along the road, picking up the pace, Leopaln began to understand his Guard Advice better. It wasn't that they were deceivers or liars, but rather that they didn't trust the officers; the Guard Advice was a blessing and a curse to Jhor. It gave her proficiency in the field, but stripped her of any accord between those that ordered and those that obeyed; if a Guard Advice distrusted an officer and he engaged a soldier more often than an officer than surely the distrust ran even deeper than most thought.

After all, a soldier was in contact with a Guard Advice from his initial day of training to either death or discharge. They listened and obeyed, taking orders because they were required to at first but later out of respect; for those that had had come from broken homes the Guard Advice became like fathers, modeling principles, morals and values, and even piety; they took faith in God as they took faith in each other. They trusted their Guard Advice and many were prepared to give their lives for them. It was said among the soldiers of Jhor that a Guard Advice was the true bayonet.

As the column raced through the rain the sounds of melee pierced the air. Mr. Kepler and his column had been overtaken on the road and had retreated into the thicket, leaving the wounded to the mercy of the savages.

"Let's go lads!" Mr. Henderson shouted, rallying the column as they charged headlong into the fight. They found the other column despairing and desperate for relief; everywhere bodies lay lifelessly as the natives hacked at limbs and went for the head. "Don't give them any mercy!"

Despite being cold from the rain, the column fixed their bayonets with fast precision and struck the bellies of their foes with wrathful vengeance; they broke jaws with the butt of their muskets and threw their adversary to the ground, trying to strangle him in the mud. They cracked skulls and put out eyes, and some even removed their bayonets and used it as a knife, slashing and thrusting it into flesh, one pushing it upwards into the chin of a native.

The blood washed away as quickly as the fighting ending, and as the natives retreated Mr. Henderson called out for his compatriot. "Mr. Kepler! Mr. Kepler!" Concern swept across his face as there came no reply, and the Guard Advice began searching among the bodies.

"Here," he said, stumbling from out of the thicket. Mr. Henderson ran over to him, as did several others, helping him up. "Is it over?"

"It is."

"Good," he said, holding his side. Blood was overflowing from it. "Damn good to hear."

"You aren't dying on me?"

"Wouldn't think of it," he said, painfully with a smile. "After all, what good is an old rock without an old tree to keep it company?" As he was cared for, Leopaln and Mr. Henderson helped retrieve the wounded and fallen. The natives had scalped a few, but otherwise had been too focused on the rest of the company.

"Damn heathens," Mr. Henderson said in disgust. "I'd run them all through, every last woman and child."

"That's uncivilized."

"These are uncivilized times, and sometimes civility depends on the edge of a blade or the end of a musket."

Chapter 11

Passing Thru the Middle Colonies

As the Marquis looked out the window at the passing countryside his mind drifted into his thoughts. How ironic it was that a nation such as Jhor could accuse its own citizens of depravity when she herself had yet to throw away the bonds of injustice; tradition was as much a part of her past and present as Fort Heritage served as a constant reminder to Clarkstown of the military arm that had quelled them.

Jhor bred inequality. Her institutions and society were rightfully advanced, proclaiming democracy in the form of a constitutional administration with Parliament and the Crown sharing in power, but as the moon never leaves the night so she remained anchored to the past. Raised from feudalistic roots, the concentration of wealth was as unusually high as the injustice that permeated into the fabrics of her society, including the law-abiding and the criminal: for unlike the commoner, accused lords received a special jury of their peers, a privilege of peerage, composed of only fellow lords, and whereas the commoner or the careless man without pedigree might be forcibly impressed into the navy a lord rarely received anything but a slap on the wrist. Such was the variation of justice.

But much worse was the fact that the aristocracy remained proudly aloof to the proletariat and peasantry, who dreamed of entering their gentry ranks but reached only as far as the bourgeoisie, who themselves pretended to hold status but only served to amuse those with more wealth for their pathetic attempts at sophistication; the décor of a home was simply unequal to the inheritance of land and wealth, no matter how exquisite or refined its hostess was. Thus, without wealth or land a citizen of Jhor could not expect to advance himself very far, for neither the ruling classes of nobles nor the average individual were without jealously; an industrial capitalist was as insecure as a simple shopkeeper, both desiring to move up in the world but simply unable to.

But if jealously were not a reason than restraint was, for the ruling classes of nobles not only controlled much of the land and wealth, but also the policies and laws of the land. Within its body of government, ambition was foiled by tradition; where a capitalist hoped to replace an aristocrat he was met with disappointment. The nobility was supreme, and smiled at its challengers; the House of Lords sat across from the House of Commons, but it may as well have been in a separate building. As one house hoped for reform the other perpetuated the status quo.

Within her halls, Parliament was as divided as the social strata. In the House of Lords sat clergymen as well as nobles, including dukes, earls, viscounts, and at the bottom of the ladder, the barons. To all, the appellation "lord" was given except for dukes and any princes of the throne. Titles were carried down generation after generation to the eldest son, and wealth was not only measured in land, but also in tenant farmers and laborers; the prefix "Sir" and "Lady" were also transmitted down, except by the class of knights and squires. They were only allowed to bear a coat of arms, but were nevertheless still considered a part of the "aristocracy."

If Parliament was a reflection of Jhor's society then it could be said her ruling minority felt nothing wrong in bearing stoic equanimity towards the impoverished, the degradation of the hard worker in a factory, or the spoliation of lands seized in warfare or through royal marriage; the Maerlese especially were made to feel the boot of exploitation and injustice, treated like any defeated party might be by its conquerors.

The Marquis sighed. Tradition was the death knell of Jhor, and yet she did not realize it. The fragility of her civilization rested at the mercy of an accident, and though she had come very close to the edge of one just recently from colonial agitation she had yet to quell it. Certainly it was only a matter of time. For it wasn't just the colonial agitator chanting reform but also her citizens too, and choosing to ignore one did not diminish the voice of the other.

Democracy was an institute of antiquity, but among the monarchies of the present day it was a dangerous notion to measure or ponder, and few if any were willing to put the responsibilities of government into the hands of the uneducated. And yet, government regardless of its form is always ruled by a minority, the Marquis thought, whether by a despot or through a plutocracy. It may boast voting by the people, but undoubtedly it would give final say to an electoral body of privileged individuals to countermand any say of the people, lest the mob rule. Democracy was an ideal of the people, but not its ruling classes, and as history had shown the will of the people is strong, but easily bent:

A properly functioning aristocracy could disguise their rule through the façade of democracy, luring the people into a falsehood with a House of Commons that could speak on their behalf. But a masterful aristocracy would go a step further and exclude certain groups of society or religion into this body of commoners, thus further limiting the power of democracy against fixed tradition; moreover, only eligible citizens could be represented and statutes of eligibility again could be narrowed to such margins as land ownership, and just how many peasant landowners were there in Jhor?

It was an unjust system, but even more detrimental was its subsequent implosive nature. If the House of Lords were moored by a strong sense of entitlement than the House of Commons was afflicted by tradition. If it wasn't jealously that impeded citizens, or the restraint by laws, or even the statutes of eligibility then it was the heritage of Jhor's feudalistic past that led to such poor representation. Population growth or decline in cities went unaccounted for, and often cities with only a few eligible voters received more representation than those with dozens. The disproportion was baffling, but perhaps even more astonishing was that half of the seats in the House of Commons were filled with uncontested nominations because the representatives came from boroughs with almost no eligible voters; buying a seat in the House of Commons went to the highest bidder.

Thus, if the citizens of Jhor were feeling the adverse effects of tradition then her colonial citizens were receiving the brunt of it. The agitators were calling for no taxation without representation, but what representative would speak on their behalf? No doubt such a seat went to the highest bidder, and so what did that person have to fear by doing nothing? Jhor was afflicted by tradition. It was killing her from the inside like a cancer, and if she continued to ignore it then it would tear her apart and her colonies would become independent.

"Let's have a rest, Nathan," he called out, in need of a reprieve from his thoughts. The carriage came to a halt and his manservant helped him down. "A beautiful day it is," he remarked, taking in a breath of fresh air. "How about a stroll?" They walked together into a field of open pasture. Happily, the Marquis leaned on his cane, taking in the landscape. "I have always loved traveling and seeing new places, but what I find most remarkable is how my breath can be taken away by just the simplest of things."

"Something is on your mind."

He chuckled. "I suppose you know me too well by now. Yes, there is. For over thirty years I have devoted my life to the betterment of my state and our people, but a man wants to know that his life's work was not in vain." He sighed. "That everything he has done has not only served a purpose but a perpetual one; to build something that one can look back on with satisfaction and not despair as it comes crashing down. I hope beyond all other hopes that what I have done will mean something and not have been for naught."

"May I speak freely?"

The Nations: Fraternity

"Please, I insist."

"Liberation is the greatest gift a man can give to another, so if nothing else endures of your accomplishments I hope you know how eternally grateful I am."

The Marquis nodded, patting him on the arm respectfully. "As it should be. You are an honorable man Nate, and I am quite pleased to have your company and council."

The two walked back to the carriage. "Whereabouts are we now?" he asked as Nate helped him back into the carriage. He suspected they were somewhere in the middle colonies given the numerous plantations they had passed, but was rather curious if they were near a major port-city.

"Near New Portsmouth. No more than a day or two. We'll stop tonight before going in."

"I shall visit the governor then."

Nate was puzzled. "You mean Governor McAlester?" If anyone was as guileful in his politics as the marquis it was J. Lamb McAlester. Neither Parliament nor the Continental Congress dared to test the man's will, whose fingers ran deep in the dirt of both sides, from rum smuggling in the colonies to court scandals and unscrupulous finances within both houses of Parliament there was enough embarrassment to shame both sides indefinitely, and so, although appointed by His Majesty as governor of the middle colonies, J. Lamb McAlester remained untouched.

Moreover, the agrarian middle of Jhor's colonies was rooted in tobacco production, a social necessity in Jhor. With such leverage and his intimate knowledge of secrets as well as strong connections on both sides of the ocean J. Lamb McAlester was able to virtually dictate terms to his benefit and those within his elite social circle; to befriend him was more than just business or politics, it was to extend an invitation into one's private affairs. Whatever the governor needed to know, or found useful about someone, he learned.

He was neither a patriot nor a loyalist but rather a patron of duplicity. He played both sides, catering to the needs of the Continental Congress for rations and munitions. He granted loans at high interest rates, but was timely in his deliveries and often generous so that the common soldier could only applaud him, thus obliging congress to continue use of his services lest they face the threat of mutiny.

As such, he was neither liked within the Continental Congress nor even Parliament for that matter. If there was one thing both sides could agree upon it was their distaste for him and his insufferable command over others. When the delegates of the colonies had met to decide whether to declare independence or not his representatives were the last to cast their vote in favor, and only did so after many concessions. Always the venture capitalist, the governor had made it explicitly clear to his delegates that if the north and south wanted their support then they would get it, but at a price… and a steep price it was, from land claims west of the mountains to mercantile and fishing rights in their waters to even command of the Continental Army.

"Indeed so, Nate. I wish to visit him."

"A man like that is dangerous. Have you met him before?"

"Of course," the Marquis replied quite astutely. "I'm the one who got him his appointment."

Chapter 12

Unfortunate News

As dawn peeked over the horizon Leopaln rested. He had survived his first engagement. Although a little shaken by it, his core was filled with a tremendous sense of pride and accomplishment. His training had paid off and he had reacted to his threats with discipline and courage.

"You did well, sir," said Mr. Henderson, sauntering over to him. "These lads have a whole new respect for you."

"I guess I have good mentors," he smiled.

"A man who learns something is better than a man who thinks he has learned everything."

"So says the philosopher stone," Mr. Kepler joked, walking over to them. He had bandaged his wound.

"Feeling any better?" Leopaln asked, shaking his hand, pleased to see his Guard Advice still intact.

"I'll live."

Leopaln was glad to have both of them; he couldn't have asked for better Guard Advice. It had been a challenging night. He had been unsure about them at first, but now realized they only had the best intentions for him and the company. After all, wasn't that the point?

"We should be getting onwards?" Mr. Kepler said. "I'll ready the men."

"Can we expect another attack?" Leopaln asked.

"From the natives? Not likely. They got a swift kick in the arse. I'd figure we're good all the way to South Anchorage Point unless we run into some rebels."

"What's the chance of that, you figure?"

"Hard to say. We're about a day's march from the middle colonies, but there hasn't been any reports of incident there; mostly from the south."

"Nevertheless, we better be prepared," added Mr. Henderson. "I suggest we do as we did before. We'll divide into two columns. With your permission of course, sir."

Leopaln could see they already thought it was a good idea and so he went along with it. As the company resumed its march, he thought back on his childhood book, about Goshen and this new world, and somehow the words had a new meaning for him. Perhaps it was that he had been in his first engagement?

When He had conquered Lameria and crossed into the lands of the Iyst, there came a hastening of cries and moans. A scathing cloud of fear loomed then over all peoples, paralyzing village and dell, towns and cities alike, all that was except one whose people dwelled upon the slopes East of the Rolan River. They defied Him and his vision…

And as the Men of Bladaria forded the great Rolan River, a hail of devastating arrows met them. Steel and shield of thousands ran to them and against the might of the river Goshen's army was broken. The great visionary lay lifeless in the water, his corpse left to the wolves, and in that year and those after the people of the Iyst celebrated His defeat in many grand festivals and banquets.

They stopped to rest at night in towns and villages along the road and continued on the following mornings without alarm. Unlike the northern colonies that were inundated with independent fervor and agitation, the sentiment in the middle colonies was more neutral. Perhaps it was just good business or simply self-preservation, but few if any saw the value in supporting the Continental Congress who had yet to achieve any decisive victory… a fact Leopaln feared about, particularly being in that battle.

Along the way, they received embraces from women and handshakes from men. Their shoes and tools were repaired and several plantations hosted a dinner for Leopaln and his Guard Advice as a thank you for their service; as they ate, Mr. Henderson regaled their hosts with stories of his adventures.

The Nations: Fraternity

And as they neared the border of the southern colonies, content and carrying full stomachs, a torrential storm all at once slowed their pace to a halt. The company sought shelter in a village, but as it carried into the night the temperature dropped and several small groups were sent to get wood. Leopaln and his group however never came back.

Chapter 13

A Straightforward Meeting

"There was an uprising in South Anchorage Point," said Governor McAlester, nonchalantly pouring himself a drink and handing one to the Marquis. "But I'm sure you were already aware of that." If he was mindful of anyone it was the Marquis; although he had learned from the best, the best was still better than he, and consequently if there was any man he feared it was the Marquis.

"Of course. Why else do you think I stopped here?"

"Or perhaps not. A man who treads too far at the edge risks falling."

The Marquis smirked at that hollow threat. His protégé still had much to learn. "I came here to inquire about your position, nothing more. I was simply curious, particularly since the Continental Congress intends to move the cause north."

"They move at my behest, not their own. I supply their wares. If and when I wish for the cause to move north then it will be so."

"The passions of men are hard to distract. I'd be more careful if I were you."

"Is that why you're here then? To warn me?"

"What need have I to warn a man who thinks he is untouchable?"

The governor took a nervous sip. He was never fond of these meetings, especially since he knew the Marquis was far more connected than he, and being reminded of that was as unsettling as the man's calm demeanor in the face of crisis. The Marquis was a master of his craft, always twelve steps ahead, and doing so without strain or sweat.

"I play both sides," the governor replied, but somehow he felt that tactic wasn't going to save him.

"Have I taught you nothing?" the Marquis said, shaking his head. He stood up and walked over to the wall to admire a painting. "You have fine taste. This is by Benito." It was an image of a dying woman clasping her child in embrace.

"Thank you," he said, hesitantly. Surely the man was about to judge him.

"What do you know of him?"

"Of Benito? Not much."

The Marquis was disappointed in that. He was more than a patron of the arts. Although he was appreciative of it, valuing each fine brush stroke such that the vision became something more than just artwork, it was also expression to him. *Caritatem Liceat Ultimum Amplexum*, Love's Last Embrace. It moved him, and brought a tear to his eyes as he remembered them. He had loved them so much, and still did.

"Benito had an apprentice," he said, not bothering to turn around. "He gave him his time and talent, and even allowed him to take credit for his own work, which not many artists did. Typically, a master artist took credit for his work and those working for him. Nevertheless, his apprentice showed promise and Benito even presented him before his Holiness, who had taken an interest in him. But ambition had blinded the young man and he became careless." He turned to face the governor. "He accused Benito of heresy and watched as the artist was seized and burned at the stake. Unfortunately, it was only then that the young man realized his fame existed so long as Benito lived, and without his master he fell into obscurity."

The governor set his drink down. "I believe our meeting is done," he said, fearing the Marquis more than ever now. "Thank you for your visit."

"I will leave when I please, Jacob," he said sharply. The tension in the room was now overwhelmingly disturbing, and as much as the governor tried to disguise his fear he knew his mentor could read right through him. "Well then, what do you want of me?"

"I want only one thing. What I asked earlier. I wish to know what position you are taking."

"You wish for me to jeopardize my investments?" he asked petrified, trying desperately to hold his ground. "I know too many secrets on both sides. That could be invaluable in the right hands."

"Do you know why they burned Benito?"

The governor had no idea. "You said it was heresy."

"No," he said calmly, "That was the excuse they used. It was because Benito was a homosexual. When his apprentice found out he tried to blackmail him, but Benito refused. So his apprentice told the authorities and the artist died for what he believed in and what he drew inspiration from; it wasn't the secret that destroyed Benito, it is what destroyed his apprentice."

"Are you threatening me, your lordship?"

"Don't flatter yourself Jacob. It doesn't paint a good picture of you."

The governor shifted uncomfortably. "So what do you want?" he asked.

"Imagery," he replied. "That's what I want from you, and I expect it very soon."

141

Chapter 14

A Hard Lesson Learned

Nate waited patiently for the Marquis outside the room. There was a painting on the wall, but he was more alert to the disdainful looks of the other three men in the room. They were glaring unkindly at him as though he didn't belong; he didn't need a soothsayer to tell him what they were thinking. The economies of the middle and southern colonies depended largely on slave labor, and though there were free Blacks, racism ran high.

"I bet you've seen the end of a whip," said one after a few minutes of silent tension. He had no reservation. "Ain't that right boy? I bet your whole back is carved up like it should be. Too much damn negro pride." The other two beside him started chuckling.

Nate just ignored them, but that only furthered the man on. He continued taunting him, mocking his wife and mother. "I bet that whore-of-a-mother of

142

yours is real proud of you, ain't she boy?" Nate squeezed his fist into a ball, but the Marquis had forbidden him to exact revenge; he had never forgotten the whip or the memory of watching his sister be beat in front of him. She had died with a look of pain and then resignation, and the man had just kept going, whipping her lifeless body even harder.

"When I speak you answer, boy!" the man now said, but Nate restrained himself. It took every fiber of his body to arrest his urge, because all he wanted to do was jump at the man and rip his limbs from his body. But now the man had had enough of his silence and walked over to him. "What are you, deaf? I said your mother is a whore, boy. So you best answer me and say she is or I will put you down!"

That was it. Nate could no longer stand it. He rose to his feet and narrowed his brow at him. His breathing hastened and his heart rate elevated; he had done nothing but mind his business, but his patience could only stand so much and this brute had to be taught a lesson.

"Don't you dare open your mouth boy," said the man, seeing him flare up. "Now you best sit down, boy."

But that wasn't going to happen. He had been pushed and no man would ever touch him again, or threaten to do so. "You have no right to threaten me," he said, still trying desperately to restrain his urges. "So, I'm giving you a choice. Either walk away or wish you had."

None of them could believe it. "Did I just hear right. Did this Negro just threaten me? Oh now you've done it, boy. Now you've gone and crossed the line. Here we were having a polite conversation of how your mama is a whore and you got to get all angry about that," he said, shaking his head. "Somebody's gonna have to teach you some manners, especially for how you're dressed. You ain't a peacock, are you boy?"

"Don't call me that."

"Call you what, boy?"

"That. Don't call me that."

"I'll call you any damn word I please," he said with a half raised lip. "Because there's not a damn thing you can do about it, boy."

He moved at him, intending to teach him a lesson, but Nate was faster and swung him to the floor. "I said don't call me that." The other two were quickly taken aback by his abrupt use of force and suddenly hesitated to join in the fray.

"You bloody peacock!" the man said, pulling himself up. If his comrades weren't going to teach Nate a lesson then by he certainly would. He drew his knife and thrust it at Nate's abdomen, but it missed as Nate threw himself back. "I'm gonna gut you, boy. You're a dead man. Nobody treats me that way.

Nobody!" He swung again, but Nate caught his arm this time and threw him to the ground again. The man quickly rose back up, but again he was dropped. "I've had just about enough of you boy," he said, infuriated beyond belief, but just then the door opened and out walked the Marquis.

"What is the meaning of this," he demanded.

"Your negro needs to be taught a lesson in manners!"

"From where I'm standing that lesson seems to have already been learned," he replied, noticing the man's stagger and apparent battering. "Now you have two choices," he said, interrupting the man from speaking again. "Either you remove yourself or hang."

"Hang! Have you lost your mind? That negro hit me!"

"I suspect he merely dodged your assaults, which were no doubt instigated by provocation, and so I again find myself repeating what I just said. Either leave or hang."

"The governor will hear of this. I have an appointment with him today."

"You have an appointment with him," the Marquis said, doubting that was true. "Well, let me enlighten you then. The governor not only knows me better, but also owes me a favor-coincidentally, a very large favor. But although I'm not as much of a gambler as you are by your mannerisms and depravity, I suspect he will no doubt acquiesce to a lesser favor of mine, which in this case would be to hang you."

The man was suddenly quiet. Speechless as he was afraid, he didn't know how to reply. The indomitability of the Marquis was as terrifying as the prospect that he probably wasn't bluffing, and so quickly and as apologetically as he could be the man excused himself.

"Did he instigate it?" the Marquis asked without turning his head. His tone was reprimanding.

"He did, and I'm sorry."

"Don't be." He despised slavery, even if society hadn't yet embraced its abolition, but what was perhaps more insufferable was racism. The Marquis could only imagine the tears from watching one's sister die, to know that the last thing she saw in this world was her brother's watery eyes and realize there was nothing he could do to save her. It was an all too familiar feeling.

Chapter 15

Meeting Henry Flemwick

"You stay silent," remarked a man, throwing Leopaln to the ground. He was too dazed and confused and when he tried to move he found his hands bound behind his back. He looked around, trying to determine where he was, but all he could see was a makeshift camp in the woods and Mr. Henderson nearby, perched against a tree. The Guard Advice was still unconscious.

About him, he could hear an argument. Apparently, he and Mr. Henderson were the topic of conversation as their captors were trying to decide what to do with them. "He's an officer. He's got to be worth something," said one.

"That there's a Guard Advice, worth twice as much," another replied. Evidently, it was a debate on ransom.

Leopaln looked about, trying to see if there was anything he might use to cut his bonds. A bit off was a knife by a campfire. He wondered if he could make it unseen, but just then one of them went over to the fire to warm up, and that's when Leopaln realized it was still raining. His hands were numb and he was shivering.

They had been ambushed while gathering wood. He quickly looked around for the soldiers in their group, but only Mr. Henderson and he were about; where were the others? Were they dead? He wasn't sure, but for the moment all that mattered was staying alive.

As he became more awake he noticed the camp was filled. There were stores of necessities everywhere. Boxes filled with salted pork or linens or munitions were scattered about; these weren't just ruffians. They were profiteers, and the worse kind at that. They had stolen the wares, killing whoever had had it, whether loyalist or rebel, and then selling it back to the highest bidder.

As he continued to look about the ruffians began to settle down for the night, choosing to wait out the storm rather than journey on. A few began to smoke, but most sat around the fire. "What about them two?" one asked, wondering if the prisoners should be kept warm.

"To hell with them," the apparent leader of the group said. "Just keep an eye on them."

The air was becoming colder and Leopaln wondered if he would survive the night. By now his coat was drenched and his whole body was shaking, verging on hypothermia. His teeth were chattering and now desperate to get warm he moved closer to Mr. Henderson.

Perching himself against the tree, he collapsed against his Guard Advice. Exhausted and cold, he closed his eyes. If he were meant to die then at least he would be with somebody he had come to trust. Time and again though he awoke, stirred by the ruffian's laugher or the frozen cold that now clung to his coat. He inched closer to Mr. Henderson and again tried to sleep, but was once again stirred awake by two ruffians who were fighting. Apparently, one had stolen the other's tobacco. He closed his eyes.

An hour later the camp was again alert and Leopaln could hear panic in their voices. Someone had spotted a search party. "I told you we should have moved," one said in a frightened voice. "There's a whole company of regulars out there searching for these two, and I ain't taking my chances with that!"

"Keep it together," the leader shouted. At once, he barked orders and the band began to load up. Everything was put on a wagon. "And get them too. We're not leaving here without them."

"They're the reason there's a whole lot of regulars out there. Forget them," one protested, but a barrel to his forehead silenced him.

"I won't say it again. Get them also."

If any escape was attempted it had to be now, thought Leopaln, but his Guard Advice was still unconscious; he had to try something, but he couldn't leave him. Unfortunately, his bonds were now even tighter from being damped. So it was useless. The more he tried to untangle, the more the rope resisted; they were grabbed and tossed towards the wagon.

"Careful with them. They're no good to us dead."

"You mean to hold us for ransom," Leopaln said, still groggy, but trying to buy some time.

"I do," the leader said.

"Running will not save you."

He laughed. "As opposed to fighting regulars. I prefer to live thank you."

"You're a coward," Leopaln said. It stung hard and drew looks from the others. "Why should they follow a coward?"

"I make them rich. That's all that matters."

"You steal from others. So, you're a thief and a coward."

"I think it's time you shut your mouth," he said, pointing his gun at Leopaln. But for the first time since having set foot in the colonies, Leopaln wasn't afraid. He had endured a barrage of insults, humiliations and shame as well as surviving an attack by natives. If he were going to die then he would go bravely. So, he just stared back at the leader and dared him to pull the trigger.

150

The Nations: Fraternity

Hidden in the thicket a young man watched the courage of the officer dare the ruffian leader. He couldn't believe it, and found himself not so much in disbelief, but rather smiling, as though he already liked him. Whoever that officer was he had indomitable courage. "Hold, all of you," he then said, bursting into the open with his gun pointed straight at the ruffian leader's head. From behind him his followers came out too, aiming their muskets at the ruffians and forcing them to surrender.

A few minutes later, Leopaln was untied and his Guard Advice was attended to. "Who are you," Leopaln asked his rescuer, finding a blanket to warm himself.

"Henry Flemwick," the energetic man said, "And whoever you are you have brass balls. Good for you."

Leopaln was a bit surprised by that, but smiled nevertheless. "Are you releasing us?"

"Of course," Henry said, "I have no reason to keep you. I came for these men."

Henry had an unusual dynamo of energy and vitality about him. He was enthusiastic and charming, earning him a certain degree of popularity in the local taverns, but also widespread fame as a high-spirited individual, laughing and spending evenings in merriment; he rarely worried, preferring instead to view the world as a source of endless possibilities.

He was an inspiring individual, drawing others to him, and whenever he took risks he did so with others, persuading them into believing that his idea was impregnable; he wasn't arrogant or demanding, but someone filled with such exuberance that others found him hard to resist. In the very best of ways, his energy was an epidemic, a joke that everyone in the pubs laughed about, and didn't stop the ladies from spending their evenings with him.

"Are you a constable?" asked Leopaln.

"Not quite. I'm a captain in the militia," he replied. He was as polite as he was appreciative for Leopaln and his Guard Advice for their service.

"You're a loyalist then?"

"Not really, but then I'm not really a rebel. I'm just not political," he said with a smile. "I figure if both sides sat down to a pint this whole mess could be sorted out."

"I suppose that's one way to look at it."

"As long as he's buying," Mr. Henderson said finally coming to. "I don't trust any man until he's either fought at my side or buys me a round."

"Well, then I suppose that makes two of us," said Henry, offering his hand. "Henry Flemwick, at your service."

"A pleasure," the Guard Advice said, accepting it, but still wary. Despite feeling a bit groggy and cold he felt obliged to intervene and ensure Leopaln wasn't falling into a trap, and so he took over the conversation. "Our party is looking for us, so I think we better be off."

"Of course," Henry said, not wishing to let them feel like prisoners again. "But I will be happy to escort you two gentlemen back to your camp in a few hours if you will allow my men to secure this camp. I feel I owe you that much."

"Much obliged, but we will take our chances."

"Perhaps we should accept," said Leopaln, overruling that. "After all, I'm famished. I think we both could eat."

"There's plenty back with the others," he pressed, but the officer was resolute.

"Mr. Henderson, I went along with your plan before. Perhaps you could extend the same courtesy to me now."

"As you wish," he said reluctantly. The sooner they were back with Mr. Kepler and the company the better; it wasn't that he didn't trust Henry a little. It was that he didn't trust him period. "But as soon as we've had a bite we're off."

"Let's extend some courtesy to Henry also," Leopaln replied, a bit scornful now. "After all, he did just save us."

"That may be," he said in an abrasive hushed tone, "but to what purpose. Until we know, I suggest you don't let your guard down."

Chapter 16

From Bad to Much Worse Tidings

As Nate sat across from the Marquis, he couldn't help but feel satisfied. He was treated with an unequal degree of humanity and empathy, and for that he was grateful; what other master treated a servant with such magnanimity? He was born into slavery and cried sometimes at night when the memories rehashed; the pain of being degraded and seeing her face was unbearable, but remembering that there was nothing he could do was even more painful and he often wailed, begging her for forgiveness.

She was in a better place now, and so was he. The Marquis was a prodigious man beset by an arduous life and dour by past memories that motivated his convictions and decisions, but beneath this epidermal armor was an undercurrent of sympathy and remorse; he was fair as he was benevolent, believing that every man was a gift to the world; he was not religious, but he did believe in a higher power, and that every wrong was judged.

He had spoken to Nate in the past about God and whether he believed in Him. Nate did, even though he harbored resentment. What had been done to his sister was unjust and had gone unpunished. What God would have allowed that? How could such evil be permitted to exist? He wondered if his tears at night were for her or the hatred he felt towards God.

"I left a note for the governor to hang that man," the Marquis said after a while of silence. "You may never find the man who hurt you or your family, Nate, but such barbarism against those in my company will not be tolerated."

Nate didn't know what to say, but then there was no need for words. He admired him and frankly agreed with his decision. After all, the man had been warned. All at once, a feeling of content spread over him and warmed his core. Justice may be barbaric, but it was well deserved.

As the carriage drove along, the Marquis now began to wonder about the news he had just been told. What might the implications be of a successful uprising in South Anchorage Point? No doubt any port the Continental Congress could acquire could mean curtailing Jhor's effort to stem the rebellion. Even with its blockade, smugglers ran rampant and with delegates abroad trying to secure loans for the Continental Congress it would only be a matter of time.

He didn't approve of their cause, but he did admire it. The unanimous Declaration of Independence by the united colonies of Jhor was as monumental a publication as it was bold. These colonial intellectuals were not simple, disgruntled peasants harboring a grudge against an oppressive master, but rather learned men, basing their principles on renaissance ideology; they weren't just dissolving the political bonds that had joined them to Jhor but were preparing to embark on a crusade of republicanism, instituting theory into practice for the whole world to judge.

They were fools, but brave ones. They were radicals, but pioneers. They were traitors, but reformers. The institutions of Jhor, her traditions as well as Parliament had evolved from absolute monarchy into a constitutional assembly with power shared between the Crown and an elected body of representatives, but as advanced as it was it still had its flaws, and this revolution not only pointed them out, but also meant to amend them with self-autonomy.

These men were business owners, lawyers, politicians, prestigious in their careers and using their education not just to advance their own lives but the lives of others; their declaration was not just for them, or any elite class, but for the status of all men in the colonies. It was a championing song for reform, trumpeted by agitators but propagated by the more tactful in courts abroad; there were voices of support coming from all corners of the world, leading patrons who believed the Continental Congress could indeed prove to the world what a republic had to offer.

"When we arrive in South Anchorage Point, I wish to visit with the commandant first," the Marquis said to Nate. He not only gave instruction for him to follow, but also found it favorable to Nate's self-esteem. It was just a theory of his, but he believed that Nate felt more empowered when he could insist upon someone, particularly against prejudice; whether it leveled the playing field or simply gave him a good feeling to be able to demand from someone who owned slaves was humorous to the Marquis; the imbalanced idea that a slave-owner might be taken aback by a colored man in a position of authority was simply too amusing to not laugh.

"I will do so, and should I also send any dispatch back to the governor?" he replied, wondering if their work with J. Lamb McAlester was completed.

"No need. The governor knows what I expect."

"May I ask what you think of our visit here so far?"

"You may always ask Nate, and I find it well-timed. We could not be in a better place at such a more perfect time."

157

That surprised him, especially with everything going on. "I would think you might wish to depart back to Aiegona for your safety. From everything I have seen and heard I feel we are about to be mixed into something big."

"Exactly why we are well-timed," he said with a hearty smile. If hardship begets resilience then tyranny always fathers revolution, and should a new nation be born then the Marquis wished to be right in the middle of it, not to celebrate its triumph, but to avert its republican proliferation into his country. Liberty was a contagious epidemic, and a venereal disease to any stable institute, poisoning its fundamentals and arousing the populace into such radicalism that it threatened anarchy; and above all else, he feared the implications of the mob running wild.... the aristocracy ruled Aiegona and he dreaded the thought of republicanism agitators calling for universal revolution. Such ferocity and aggressiveness could only be checked with bloodshed, but in so doing would arouse internal dissent, prompting widespread riots and looting. Against such liberal radicalism what chance did stability have?

"How ironic fate it is," the Marquis said, musing.

"What is?"

"Freedom. It is a fickle thing."

Chapter 17

On the Road Again

All night, Mr. Kepler and the company searched, but by morning they were soaked, cold and exhausted and had to rest. Though still determined, they closed their eyes for an hour; they wanted to find them just as much as Mr. Kepler. They were as worried about their welfare as well as their safety, and many even expressed concern for Leopaln, who they now trusted a bit more.

"We will leave, but not yet. Get some more rest," Mr. Kepler said, reluctantly taking his own advice. He too wanted to continue the hunt, but they didn't know what to expect and so everyone needed to regain their strength.

An hour later, a rider came galloping down the road and was surprised to find a company of regulars. At once, he burst into praise. "Thank the Heavens," he said jubilantly.

Mr. Kepler received him curiously, but upon hearing his news he regretted it. All at once a grave look spread across his face as he was suddenly faced with a hard decision. There had been an uprising in South Anchorage Point and now it had boiled over. Supported by the rebels, the city was under siege; the commandant had issued a desperate plea for reinforcements and had sent his fastest rider to Fort Heritage.

"We're from there," Mr. Kepler told the man, who almost hugged him. "But we can't leave yet."

The rider took a step back. What, why not?" What was more pressing than answering this call for help? He didn't understand. "But surely, there is nothing of greater importance?"

The Guard Advice nodded. He understood the gravity of the situation, but he couldn't leave without Mr. Henderson or Leopaln or the men they were with. "We're conducting a search for some missing people. When we find them then we will respond with all due haste."

The rider tried to protest, but Mr. Kepler would not listen. He was well aware of what was at stake, but he could not abandon anyone. "When we find them, then we will proceed as I said."

"If you find them," the man replied. His joy was now all but gone. As he rode off, Mr. Kepler turned around to see the company ready to go. They would not wait another second.

"Alright," he said, appreciating their resolve, "let's start looking again."

Elsewhere, Henry was escorting Leopaln and Mr. Henderson, but not in the direction they expected.

Chapter 18

Having Good Reasons

By noon it became apparent that they were being misled. "And you wanted to trust him?" whispered Mr. Henderson, but Leopaln just ignored him. If that was indeed the case then why, he wondered. What motive could Henry possibly have for deceiving them? Unless of course he was in fact a rebel, and they had simply fallen into another rival faction that wished to pocket the ransom.

"You mean to hold us captive?" he asked, interrupting the tranquility. "Why else would you be taking us in the opposite direction?" Suddenly, everyone came to a halt.

"You're not in chains, are you?" Henry replied indifferently. He neither felt personally offended by the accusation nor bothered by it.

"Then why haven't we reached the town yet? Our men are waiting for us, if not already searching for us."

"That's because we're not going there. We're headed south, not east."

"What, why?" he protested, reluctant to be wrong about trusting him when his Guard Advice didn't.

"Because," he added, "we're making a quick stop first. I promised you, and I'm a man of my word."

"Where to?" Mr. Henderson now said, interrupting.

"Lamsburg. It's a small town just a few days ahead."

"Why there?"

"Business."

"You have no right to take us with you!"

"And I have made no insistence that you should," he replied, still not offended. "I simply have requested your company."

"Very good," he said, grabbing Leopaln and pulling him away. "Let's go."

"But before you go," Henry quickly added, "please know I cannot protect you once you leave, and you really shouldn't be alone, not in these parts."

"We'll take our chances."

"Please," he begged. "I mean no disrespect, but the men you came with are dead. If they couldn't protect you then how do you expect to survive? I can protect you, but we need to make this stop first."

"And how do you expect to protect us?"

"Well, for starters, I wouldn't suggest wearing red in the woods," he said frankly. He and his men wore dark colors to hide themselves.

It was a good point, and Leopaln silently had to agree with that, but he took pride in what he wore, and if he died then at least he was dressed in the colors of his homeland. Nevertheless, he felt his uniform had easily distinguished him from his surroundings, giving him away to the ruffians earlier.

But there was something else. For the first time since he had arrived in the colonies, Leopaln felt he could trust a colonial. There was something about Henry that was both unusual as well as uncanny. Perhaps it was his impartiality or apparent indifference to the revolution; he had yet to show any signs of sympathy towards the Continental Congress, so whatever his intentions Leopaln felt he at least owed him some measure of gratitude; he doubted Henry was as unscrupulous as his Guard Advice wished to believe, and instead wished to give him the benefit of the doubt.

But what in the small town of Lamsburg could be so pressing as to demand his attention? Moreover, why worry his guests in accompaniment? If Leopaln had not asked he may never have known. Did Henry not realize his guests were as suspicious as they were wary?

"When I make a promise I keep it," Henry added. "Besides, I'm sure both of you could use a bed and some hot food, and if you don't mind I'd like to cover the bill. It's the least I can do for your troubles."

"How noble," Mr. Henderson said, still cynical.

"Would you do me a favor then," Leopaln asked, accepting his magnanimity. "Could you send a rider to the town and let my company know we will meet them in Lamsburg?" Henry saw no issue with that and nodded.

Chapter 19

Pomp and Circumstance

Whatever quandaries the colonies gave Parliament it was nothing compared to the insufferable arrogance of Lord Horwick, whose egotism was beyond intolerable. Haughty and full of self-importance, he excused the ambassador sent to discuss terms of peace with Romennal. "If and when I feel they are sufficiently beaten, I shall conduct terms myself," he said. "Thank you for coming and good-bye."

When threatened with court-martial, he just laughed. He was a monarchist, and he came from a proud lineage of aristocratic loyalists to the Crown; his grandfather had not only been a royalist in the great feud between His Majesty and Parliament at the turn of the century, but had also helped to finance it; when the Maerlese had joined Parliament to check the power of the Crown they were undone, and his grandfather had played a significant role in   that.

The Nations: Fraternity

And though power was eventually shared, Lord Horwick always considered that to have been His Majesty's decision not Parliament's. He had no respect for Parliament or its flawed notion of democracy. To him, it was filled with scandalous morals and inefficiency, nothing more than a cabinet of shreds and patches trying to be worn.

To him, the monarchy was the purest measure of efficiency and for pushing social change forward. When Parliament protested the Crown's confiscation of Church property and assets, the people lost out on new public works; when royal decrees that supported the religious minority for government posts were rebuked the populace lost out again on productive men. At every step, Parliament was nothing more than a brat child, demanding more power than the Crown. Meanwhile, the people suffered under the tyrannical yoke of their incompetence. No wonder why he was a monarchist. He reviled Parliament and its deficiencies.

He was a man of pedigree, noble in every sense of the word, and admonished colonials as much as he loathed Parliament. When he was finished in Romennal, he intended to crush the rebellion once and for all; peasants should know their place. As God picked His Majesty to rule, so the bottom dwellers should be content with the scraps.

"Sire," a Guard Advice interrupted. "Our reports indicate Romennal has marshaled a large army. What are your orders?"

He looked at the man with contempt. "Why am I being bothered with peasants armed with pitchforks? A sergeant could brush those lambs aside." He longed for a test of his brilliance and wit, but not even the might of Romennal had given him that. He had rolled their disciplined armies over like they were papers falling off a desk; his capture of Voggénlor was more a joke than a siege. He yearned for a real challenge, a contest between titans, and he had expected to find it in Romennal. Perhaps it was not meant to be though. As God had picked His Majesty to rule, perhaps it was that God had also chosen him to be the best among men on the battlefield. Such was fate.

Chapter 20

At the Crossroads of the Colonies

Leopaln had developed a bad cough and was now placed in the wagon. His body was shivering and he was running a fever. "Your officer needs a doctor," Henry said with great concern. The Guard Advice appreciated his sympathy, but still distrusted him. "Then let's pick up the pace," he replied.

Along the way, they stopped to pick up supplies and eat a warm meal, but Leopaln had to be fed. He was far too weak now; he could hardly stand let alone hold a spoon. Whatever water he drank his body still needed more. "How much further to Lamsburg?" the Guard Advice asked.

"A few more days."

"That's what you said a few days ago!" he said, suddenly agitated. "Do not lie to me. If he dies, so do you!"

"I assure you, we are near."

Lamsburg was known as the Crossroads of the Colonies, because it lay at the intersection of the Merchant Road and Sterling Way, a thoroughfare that was the southern colonies' counterpart to the former. A commercial venue, it was as busy with trade as it was an artery for gossip; there were more inns in Lamsburg than in any other city. If anyone wanted news about something Lamsburg was the place to be. But housing a plurality of sympathies often meant feelings boiled over into brawls, and just as liberals and conservatives disputed in the houses of Parliament so too did loyalists often argue with rebels in the inns, making it both a lively place of debate as well as a breeding ground for violence.

"I will hold you to that," he replied in a threatening manner. All that mattered to Mr. Henderson then was rejoining Mr. Kepler, and the sooner the better. With Leopaln's health declining and in the company of suspicious characters, Mr. Henderson hardly slept a wink. They were supposedly Henry's guests, but he seriously doubted that.

Henry was too indifferent. He was lively and energetic, but this was war and knowing whom to trust was everything. He neither showed inclinations towards the loyalists nor gave any remarks to the rebels; whatever he talked about was anything but politics. It was as though he was either oblivious to current events or simply undecided at the moment on which side to choose, and a neutral party, especially armed, could be as dangerous as an enemy. And if there was one thing Mr. Henderson distrusted more than anything else it was neutrality.

Two days out, they stopped again to rest. Leopaln's condition was only worsening. Despite every blanket and as much water as they could put down his throat it still wasn't enough. His fever had not yet abated and now every second counted. "Let's get going," Mr. Henderson ordered. Henry agreed and the rest was cut short.

"I'll send a rider ahead," he offered, trying once again to earn his guest's trust. Despite every attempt of hospitality, the Guard Advice only furthered distanced himself away, but Henry was undaunted. He valued a good challenge and tried to make conversation whenever he could.

"So, where have you seen service?"

"Let's stay focused," he replied coldly.

"I'm just curious."

"And I'm not interested in talking."

Anyone else might retreat, but not Henry. "As you wish. I'll do the talking."

"What don't you understand? I don't want to talk and that also means listening to you, so find someone else, because I have other affairs that need attending to."

Henry looked around, bemused by that. "What other affairs? I see only us and the road ahead."

But that only thinned the man's patience "Why don't you go bother somebody else!"

"As you wish, but let me say one last thing."

"For bloody sake's, what?"

"Thank you."

Now it was the Guard Advice who was baffled. "For what?" What could Henry possibly be thanking him for?

"You probably don't hear it much nowadays, but thank you for your service." It was the first comment of politics he had made, and it was the last thing Mr. Henderson had expected. He wanted to question that, not sure whether to believe him or not, but something about Henry's face and the way he said it inferred he probably meant it.

"Well, just doing my job," he said, trying not to let his guard down. It was a nice compliment. In fact, as he thought about it, he had never received that type of compliment from anyone but officers and foreign civilians.

"Well, I certainly do appreciate it, and for what it's worth I'm honored to have your company. After all, how often does one get the opportunity to spend time with the legendary Guard Advice?"

"Well, we all have a job to do," he said hesitantly, "and I try to do the best I can."

"Is it difficult?"

"Is what difficult?"

Henry paused a moment. "Is it difficult being here in the colonies?" For a second the Guard Advice wavered. He was about to speak, but the way Henry asked it made him rethink his response. There was empathy in his voice, as though he was trying to understand the perspective from both sides instead of the narrow-minded agitators.

"Yes, it can be," he said, being a bit more open. "But no more dangerous than anywhere else."

"But you don't get hostility like you do here. We're supposed to be brethren, but when I saw those criminal ruffians looking at you and your officer that wasn't family. That wasn't one people united. It was adversity of the worst kind, like a family torn in two." There was sadness in his voice. "How can anywhere else be more difficult than here? Men turn on one another here, good men, men that I've trusted and who I'd die for."

"You know them?" he asked, surprised. "You know those ruffians that we captured us."

"I do," he said reluctantly, ashamed to say it. The captured men were still with them, but kept in the rear. "He was my lieutenant... and my neighbor." He couldn't believe he was admitting it. "I know his wife and their children. How can I tell her that I put a gun to her husband's head, a man that I've

173

known for years? How do you look her in the face and tell her that? And if he is to hang for his crime then how do you live with that? If it's difficult for you being here, it's even more difficult living here."

Mr. Henderson hadn't realized that. Suddenly, he had a whole new respect for him. All this time, he suspected Henry was simply deceiving them, conniving some scheme, but now he realized the truth was far from that. Henry was just in hiding. He was an energetic, enthusiastic person, but only to hide the torment that embroiled within him; he was at war with his conscience, and though he hadn't picked a side yet it was only a matter of time before he did, and perhaps that was the most dangerous part about it: a man who can turn on his neighbors is a danger to both himself and others.

"We have to make choices. He made his."

"I wish that was true," he said, "but I was a school teacher. I taught his boy just like others. I taught them mathematics and philosophy. I taught them right from wrong. I tried giving them some sense of morals and values, but I guess I did my job too well." He shamed himself. "You fill somebody's head with liberty and this is what you get. I wanted to make a difference."

"You did your job, but you can't be responsible for their actions. As I said, that's on them."

"But how do you pull the trigger then?"

"Easy, point and shot."

"I'm a teacher first, a captain second. I fill brains, not empty them."

"Then I'll do it," Mr. Henderson said, holding out his hand to have his pistol. "If you can't then I will. This is war, and whether you like it or not some things have to be done. You call him your neighbor, but I call him a public enemy and there's no room for laws in war. So, either you do it or I will."

Henry weighed the decision. How far down the road did he have to go to be as cold as the Guard Advice? How much of him had to be sacrificed to look his neighbor in the eyes and pull the trigger, knowing the man was leaving behind a wife and kids? "I can't do it."

"Why not? I hear you barged right in when we were still captured? You didn't hesitate then. What if something had happened? Would you have pulled the trigger then?"

"That's different."

"How so?" he asked, indifferent to the idea of killing a man in cold blood. "I'll let you in on a little secret. Killing is no different than teaching. A lesson is always learned, whether you're the man pulling the trigger or feeling the cold clutch of death take you as your heart stops. In war, it's either him or you.

The minute you let compassion rule your decisions you've let death walk through the front door."

"They should be tried for their crime."

"This is war. You're judge, jury and executioner. Now do what needs to be done." Henry hesitated, but the Guard Advice was adamant. If Henry couldn't do it then he would, and he would have no qualm about it; he had killed before and would do it again without remorse.

The group halted and Henry pulled out his pistol. He walked back to the ruffian leader, who all at once began begging for his life. He pleaded with him, apologizing for everything and asking for a second chance; he started to cry, unwilling to accept the horrific truth that his wife was about to become a widow as a result of his own blind ambition.

"You don't have to do this," the man cried, entreating him to reach into his heart for some degree of humanity. Henry paused, faltering in his decision. He still saw a good man and began to reconsider, but all at once a shot rang out and the man collapsed dead. From behind him the Guard Advice had done what was needed, what he could not, and what he had been meaning to do since they had been rescued. Having quickly grabbed a pistol from one of Henry's men he fired it without falter.

"Next time, don't hesitate."

"That was a good man! He didn't need to die."

"He meant to ransom us. Yes, he did."

"But he begged for his life!" Henry retorted.

"I wouldn't have," he replied, unsympathetically. The Guard Advice had done his job, at least in his mind. He was a soldier, not a civilian, and death came with the territory; the first time he killed it tore him asunder, but now it was second nature. "This is war," he said unremorsefully. "I do what is necessary to survive; I don't hesitate. If you're at a crossroads with your conscience then you're already dead."

Chapter 21

The Demons Within

Upon receiving word of Leopaln's missing, the captain threw down a bookcase, shattered a mirror and threw everything off his desk. From afar, his attendant watched with worry and dread and only intervened when the captain placed his pistol into his mouth; his one and last true friend was gone, and all at once his world was collapsing; what point was there in living? The irrevocable loss of Leopaln was too much to bear.

"Be gone with you!" he shouted at his attendant, who desperately tried to wrestle it away. "I must be allowed to do this." He threw the man to the floor and pointed it at him. "I must be allowed to end this torment. Don't you understand?" he said, unable to bear the excruciating pain any longer, as though the demons were toying with him, laughing merrily at his loss. He had to end it. "I must! And not you, nor God himself will stop me." He placed the gun to his temple, and for a second contemplated following through. Then he wept.

The Nations: Fraternity

Every memory of Leopaln came rushing at him, and he suddenly felt weak, overcome with a feeling of paralyzing helplessness. He couldn't do it. Even in his worst agony, he couldn't pull the trigger. He stared up at the ceiling then, looking for a sign. "Oh God, why? Why have you hurt me?" He said aloud, tears streaming down his face. "Why have you cursed me so? Why have you taken away the one shining light in my life? I have been your loyal servant. What more must you ask of me to prove my faith? I am yours." He stood awaiting an answer, but none came, and so he collapsed into his chair, the pistol falling from his hand onto the floor, and there he sat rejected, despondent and lost.

He could no longer restrain the torment. If the Heavens would not answer him, then perhaps the Devil would. He surrendered to the demon inside of him, allowing it to peel away his soul. He did not deserve Heaven, and Hell was too good for him; Purgatory was where he belonged. He closed his eyes then and dreamed of standing in front of Fort Heritage, shaking hands with the dead. They were either greeting him or bidding him adieu. He did not know which, but they were wishing him well; and for the first time, he felt welcomed and at peace. A serene tranquility warmed him, and as he went down the line shaking hands, he felt content. There was no rebellion, no animosity, no agitators or politics, just a place to call home and friends to share eternity with.

All at once, he felt a great weight lifted, the passing of worries, and at once he felt alive, rekindled with new spirit. He took a deep breath and awoke to a renewed sense of vibrancy and energy; the tears were gone and he found himself laughing, but not out of joy or merriment, but in union with something dark. He chuckled. It wasn't the hands of the fallen that he had been shaking, but the demons he was embracing.

Chapter 22

The Tavern at Lamsburg

As they neared Lamsburg, Henry did all the talking to whoever passed by and questioned the group. To prevent too many inquires, Mr. Henderson was given a new coat to disguise his identity, and although he was displeased by the idea of hiding from the enemy Leopaln was in no shape to fight. So, the less attention they drew the better.

Lamsburg was rife with rebellion. Having no expectation except for gossip, gambling and the gathering of perfidy it was the last place any loyalist wished to be, and as quietly as they could Henry secured a doctor who could be trusted. "You brought him here?" the physician asked, dumbfounded. "He'll be dead before morning."

"Do what you can doctor," he said, knowing the risks. "I'll worry about his safekeeping."

"Then it's your funeral too. Why did you bring him here? I can help him, but for

God's sakes to what point? The instant he is discovered his fate is sealed; you could have sent for me on the outskirts. At least then I'd feel like my patient has a chance at living!"

"I appreciate the concern, but he's my responsibility and I'll make sure he walks out of here."

Leopaln was staged in a room with two men to watch him. "I'll watch him too," Mr. Henderson said, stubbornly.

"No, I need you to accompany me," Henry said.

"Like hell I will."

"Do you remember I told you I was coming here on business? Well I need your assistance with that." He paused abruptly. "This may sound strange, but there is nobody else I can trust with this errand except you." That was unexpected.

"You're bloody joking."

"I wish I was, but none of my men would be any good in this meeting. They don't have a lot of worldly experience. They're good men, but they're farmers or tradesmen. Most of have never left their own county; for many this is the furthest they've ever been from home!"

"What kind of meeting is this?" he asked perplexed. "And who exactly are we meeting?"

"A foreigner."

"A foreigner?" Well this wasn't strange at all. "Why are you meeting a foreigner in Lamsburg?" He asked, not liking any of this one bit. After all, it wasn't as if Henry was a high-level negotiator between nations; why would any foreigner wish to meet with a captain of the militia? None of this made any sense. "Alright, say I go with you. What exactly do you need from me in this meeting?"

Henry hesitated to answer. For someone who balked at danger he was sufficiently frightened. "I don't know what to expect when I go in there, so I'd like to have another person with me, someone whose appearance could tip the scales in my favor."

Mr. Henderson chuckled. "You want me to intimidate them is that it?" Henry nodded. "Alright, lead the way."

As Leopaln rested, the two headed for the Ruddy Wheel Mead Hall, a tavern known for its erosion of civilization, attracting every low-life scoundrel, knave, degenerate gambler, and hooligan. Located on the edge of town, it was a cesspool of depravity that only the bravest or most foolhardy ventured; erected along an aged stone fence its exterior was disheveled, giving it an ominous feeling, and its atmosphere inside did nothing to stem that dread. It was as loud as it was unruly, scaring the pious with its boisterous clamor. But to Henry it was a welcomed dare. How a foreigner unnerved him but the gutter of humanity did not was as much a mystery to him as the curious looks of everyone when Mr. Henderson stepped in.

At once, every gaze was upon him, stabbing him with poisonous glares. As rancid as the air smelled from a blend of unwashed bodies and tobacco its occupants were even less tidy in their attire, bearing as many scars and unkindly expressions as they had knives and pistols about them; all at once, a few hands reached for their weapons. It wasn't that they recognized him as a Guard Advice, but rather for the simple reason that he looked like a northerner trying to mingle in with the wrong crowd:

As much as the Continental Congress wished to believe that every state was united in its crusade the fact was nothing divided the country more; although the fight for independence from Jhor was inevitable, whether now or in perhaps twenty years, it was northern agitation that fueled the already disenchanted sentiment brewing: heavy levies was one thing, but what incensed the northern elite most of all was the restriction on westward expansion. There were always loopholes in taxes, but to be prohibited from developing larger estates or speculating into commercial ventures such as minerals and furs was intolerable; without new opportunities it was no surprise than that the loudest agitators were the ones who owed the most to creditors.

The Nations: Fraternity

But whereas the North drove forward, the South remained happily stagnant, celebrating its old-fashioned customs without haste. While one polar end spoke their mind the other retained a polite reservation of opinion, observing etiquette above all else, as though it were a commandment; in the North, businessmen hosted dinners to network, speaking out of turn and presenting just enough manners to not disgust their guest. In the South, decorum presided over everything, from dinners to dances, patronage of the arts, the opera, and equestrian spectacles.

Being cordial was as just as important in the South as giving thanksgiving. Even the slave-servant dispensing wine into a glass was valued for her place in society; it was an expression of tradition, gratitude and tragedy, tragic in the sense that if she were to accidently miss the glass she would be whipped unmercifully: courtesy was to know one's place and know one's task well. The slaves worked and the social elite hosted.

But the northerner did not understand this mentality nor did he wish to. Although abolitionism was a minor voice in politics to many slavery had no place in an ever-changing world: whereas the northerner viewed independence with commercial optimism and economic growth the southerner hoped to preserve its heritage. It had no need for entrepreneurs like the north; it had no need to incentivize its workforce. It was happy where it was and had no wish to change and although southerners joined the Continental Army in besieging South Anchorage Point they camped separately, taking time to eat their meals, and cordially refused to take orders from anyone but a southerner. They even offered to host dinner to the besieged commandant.

And so as Mr. Henderson stepped in and was abruptly caught by surprise by everyone staring at him, preparing to judge him on his hospitality- whether he would greet them or simply mind his business- his silence was suddenly and fortunately saved by Henry. "Evening," he said, extending warm wishes to all. "I hope everyone is doing quite wonderful." That sufficed and as everyone turned away Henry looked over to him. "Next time, don't hesitate."

Chapter 23

Imagery and Reprisals

The governor poured himself another drink. Imagery. That was what the Marquis had asked of him, but as he stared at the painting by Benito he contemplated how exactly he might achieve that to his ends; whatever course of action he took had to benefit him more, and if there was one thing J. Lamb McAlester knew how to do well it was making sure he benefited. He played both sides, but in the end he always came out on top- allegiances were overrated- and although he owed the Marquis his position he felt gratitude should be parceled and never doled out in one thanksgiving.

"Lawton," he said, calling for his aid. The man came over to him, awaiting orders. He was compliant and loyal, the way J. Lamb McAlester preferred his attendants.

"My lord," he said, ready to fulfill any request.

"What makes a man great isn't what he does, Lawton, but those who follow him, and what I need now more than ever is willingness and unquestionable commitment."

"You have it, my lord."

He smiled. "I am pleased to hear that, but I doubt that everyone is as committed as you to my services. Our borders are fraught with insurrection, and without protection- except for our militias- I am afraid that the future is bleak at best. We are undone."

"Should I cease all transits?" he asked, wondering if the governor meant to end his support of the Continental Congress.

"Not at all. In fact, I mean to double the order."

"My lord? Surely that would be noticed?"

"Indeed, it will be. But loyalty in times like these test our principles, challenging us to triumph in the name of a greater cause. Imagery, the process by which something bigger than ourselves is created, and perhaps with your help we can do that."

"Of course, my lord," he answered eagerly.

"Good. Now assemble the militia."

"My lord? To whom are we attacking?" he asked, puzzled by that last order. Hadn't the man just got done talking about aggregating his support for the revolutionaries? Why was he now all of a sudden changing his mind and wishing to assemble the militia? To whom were they going to fight or defend against? Lawton was confused.

"The militia, Lawton. Have them assembled now."

"But my lord, we are without leadership," he said, politely forgiving his boldness. It was true though. The captain had been chasing a band of ruffians that had robbed a transit caravan on its way to the congress. "Without Henry who is to lead them? Begging your pardon, but shouldn't we wait for his return and any news?"

"The captain is attending to past matters, and I am attending to the current. Ready the militia."

"As you wish, my lord."

"And Lawton," he added. "Dispatch them north."

The man looked puzzled. "But my lord, what if Captain Flemwick is in the south? He may be caught. Perhaps we should send for him."

But he was cut off. "My nephew can handle himself."

"As you wish, but why to the north if I may ask? Isn't the rebellion currently engaged in the south?"

"It is, but that is not our concern is it?"

"No my lord," he replied, taking the implication. "I suppose not."

Indulging in colonial politics was both an art and skill, and those engaging in its gladiatorial arena either came out on top or followed someone who did. J. Lamb McAlester prided himself as the former, leveraging his agenda by hook or by crook, and caring little for those who lives he tarnished along the way. It wasn't personal, well sometimes it was... considering the secrets he carried.

But then he did what he did simply because he could. So what if he ruined someone else's career: chances were the person deserved it; debauchery and lewdness were as rampant in their sexual proliferation as much as greed corrupted, and it didn't take an ancient philosopher holding a lamp during the daytime to know that the world had fewer honest men in it. So, if anything he was doing a public service by shining light on the infidelities of other's immorality, and thus he justified his loyalty.

He had ruined so many lives of those whose political careers were blossoming, or were in full bloom; the wives of those he had ruined damned him, cursing his name, and wishing to have remained in the dark than live on the street. But he felt no sympathy for them, except that they had married an immoral soul. J. Lamb was called cold-hearted, but he preferred the term, upstanding. And now as the Marquis bade him to fashion imagery, he pondered how to do so delicately. This would require much finesse, such as to avoid the reprisal of the resentful as well as the unforgiving political machinations from those that continuously sought to return the favor and destroy him and his career.

"And Lawton," he added, "don't bother sending for my nephew."

Chapter 24

Chapter 24

Jehannette-Marie

Arrah Evelyn was beside herself upon learning the presumed death of Leopaln. His reported disappearance had been swiftly carried across the ocean, and as she poured her heart into a handkerchief, Leopaln's father stood over her. "Such news is dreadful," he said, sharing her sympathy, "and I am heavy in my heart for this loss as well. A father should never have to bury his son."

She embraced him then, sharing his despair. "I'm so sorry for you." He patted her back lovingly, appreciating her empathy. "Be calm, my child," he said, offering her assurances. "We shall endure this; I shall endure this, but we must be strong now, and raise our heads. We must persevere, even in the face of death, for our lives must go on, and we must make good on whatever promises we held to him."

She sunk her head into his chest, feeling his heartbeat, and allowing herself to believe him. "I want to, but it is too hard."

"You must. We both must."

"But how does one go on living?" she asked, ignoring the tears still streaming down her face.

"Because that's what he would want. I loved my son more than anything, and I promised him before he left that I would look after you." She raised her head, amazed at his blessing.

"God bless you, my lord. Thank you."

He folded his arms around her, completing the embrace. "You are quite welcome, my dear. He loved you and I shall love you now as a daughter." His words warmed her and she gave thanks to Heaven for his kindness.

"I cannot thank you enough."

"It is what my son would have wanted," he said, offering a smile. She smiled back, embracing him tighter for his love and devotion to his son's memory. Truly, he was a good man and as noble a father as one could be. "Now may not be the most appropriate time," he suddenly said, "but please forgive me a moment."

He excused himself, letting her embrace go, and headed to a door at the end of the room. There he opened it slightly ajar, and partially exiting, he talked with someone on the other end. Then he returned. "When I learned of the news I thought only of your wellbeing, and if I may be so bold, I wish to further your education as a lady."

She was shocked, unable to believe how gracious his heart was for her. "Ms. Evelyn, may I present to you a distinguished colleague and friend of mine, Ms. Jehannette-Marie." At that, a tall, slender woman entered the room and greeted Arrah with the charm and grace of a queen. Her taste in attire was as exquisite as her jewelry, which was the envy of all kings.

"It is a pleasure to meet you Arrah," she said, taking her new pupil aside. "I can see you're already a beautiful woman, and though I'm sad for your loss, I hope that together we can build a friendship that will give you strength."

Arrah was overjoyed and again cried, but this time tears of joy. "I don't know what to say to both of you, but thank you. My heart is heavy, but also grateful." She tried wiping away the tears and collecting herself. "I guess I'm a mess," she chuckled.

"It is our pleasure," he said, accepting her gratitude. "I have lost a son, but I'd like to think I have gained a daughter, and I promise you I will do everything in my power to ensure your future is looked after."

Chapter 25

The Governor's Wife

J. Lamb McAlester owed much to the Marquis, but though he wished to deny it he owed even more to his wife, or ex-wife, Jehannette-Marie. If anyone was his equal counterpart, it was she. The envy of eyes, she was beautiful, stately, and seductive in her grace; her gaiety and charm empting more state secrets than could be guarded. Her gentle strength espousing an aura of innocence and purity, but beware the wolf in sheep's skin! Vibrant and full of life, she was cunning as she was relentless; a formidable ally in matrimony, she was unforgiving and ruthless in divorce.

Not to be underestimated, her network was extensive, owing largely to him, but now she could stand alone having discovered her own potential, and now neither Parliament nor His Majesty ignored her presence. In fact, they delighted in her social company and contributed extensively to her penchant of finding homes for stray cats; a champion of philanthropy, she earned the adulation of the public as well as the flattery of the southern colonial elite for her impeccable taste and exceptional parties.

And of all of his ministers, His Majesty valued her opinion most of all, taking pleasure in walks with her through his gardens; she was tactful but spoke with candor, and he appreciated that. He trusted her, and thanked her for her visits. Sometimes, they played chess or cards, but always he made time for her, weighing her view with the highest regard; he warmly embraced the scientific opinion of the times that the female creature was inherently unthreatening, and that her opinion would always carry a "motherly" virtue.

And although she had no children by birth, she accepted her nephew as her own. Following the death of her sister at childbirth, she took the boy as her own, raising him and praising his magnanimity towards others. Henry was a good boy, and she looked out for him.

"Thank you, Aunt Jehannette," he had said to her after learning she had secured him a post as schoolteacher a few years back.

"Even after all these years you still call me aunt," she said happily. "You know you can call me mom, Henry. It's okay." He knew he could, but he never did. He reserved that title to the mother he never knew. "My sister would be proud of you," she said. "You have become a strong man, compassionate and understanding, and you certainly have my sister's passion for danger. I'll never understand either of you; you leap at it like you expect it to cower before you," she said amazed. As much as it worried her, she loved him even more for it. "I'm glad you have it though," she smiled. "It reminds me of her."

She loved Henry as her own, and although she had often been away during his childhood, helping her then husband with his politics, she spent every second with Henry upon her return. She played games with him and schooled him in his education; he was tutored by private mentors, and learned to socialize early on, pleasing her when he became the focal of attention at her parties: it was not uncommon for little Henry to be surrounded by plantation owners, lawyers, doctors, auction house directors, and shipping proprietors.

As Henry grew up he became a favorite of the southern colonial elite, and they jumped at the opportunity to brighten their shining star. They opened their homes to him, giving him tours of their plantations, the slave quarters, and coaching him on the value and importance of accountability: slaves were an essential part of the economy, but it was the burden of the master to care for them, to tend to their needs, and cultivate a sense of civilization out of the animal; it was natural, they explained, for a beast to resist, and so it was necessary to castigate, sometimes with extreme measures, in order to rectify improper behavior and implant civil virtues.

And although she exposed her son to slavery, she neither owned one nor expected him to become an abolitionist. Instead, she intended to increase his chances of success in life by giving him connections to resourceful people; it was what she believed her sister would want.

To give Henry every advantage in life was her never-ending goal, and he never failed to impress her, whether teaching or joining the militia, or even when J. Lamb divorced her, claiming all assets and Henry as his own, and attempted to drive her into a nunnery. Henry stood by her, and although he respected his surrogate father, he had never loved him as much as he did her.

"That boy is mine, Jehannette!" he asserted loudly, throwing her out. He had no love for the boy and only meant to spite her. She had become too powerful in her exchanges, learning to stand on her own, and J. Lamb felt threatened by that and meant to reduce her. "You exceeded your natural state, which is to be my second," he told her, belittling her and threatening to expose her most coveted secrets to the world if she dared defy him.

"If I were you I'd spend the rest of my days in a nunnery, because the only networking you'll be able to do now will be with the scum of the Earth out of a bed!" And although it was her darkest hour she still had friends in high places, and even Henry supported her, giving her nearly everything he earned; J. Lamb threatened to destroy him too, but the boy gladly accepted the invitation and J. Lamb backed down.

It was for these reasons that J. Lamb McAlester stared at Benito's painting and pondered imagery. The master. The apprentice. His wife had learned from him, and he from the Marquis, but what of Henry? What of this boy who didn't fear him, who seemingly feared nothing? How was he supposed to handle him? He neither considered him his son nor even his nephew, but minimizing him couldn't erase the fact that he was related to him. And J. Lamb abhorred that fact.

Whereas Jehannette-Marie had been under his thumb, whether abroad or at home, indulging in fanciful tastes, costly jewelry and extravagant wardrobes as she networked, Henry could not be leashed. Whenever J. Lamb tried to attach strings to a gift, bribe him, or even blackmail him, Henry just became disappointed, as though he expected a greater challenge out of him.

As Lawton left the room to assemble the militia, J. Lamb contemplated his next move. Imagery. A smug then suddenly spread across his face. Oh, he would give him imagery. He would undo that woman he had married and if Henry wanted the challenge of a lifetime then he would gladly give him one. That boy would learn.

Chapter 26

A Secret Rendezvous

Back in the tavern, Henry and the Guard Advice approached a table set against the back wall where a stranger and his manservant sat. There they were greeted with southern hospitality and gestured to sit. "Thank you for coming," the Marquis began, "or perhaps I should simply say good evening as your arrival was expected."

"Who are you," asked Mr. Henderson, baffled. The man looked familiar, but he couldn't place it.

"I am the Marquis de Eliám."

"And to what purpose are we here this evening?"

The aristocrat smiled. "Although you do not know me, my good sir, someone else at this table does." His eyes wandered over to Henry. "We have no need for secrets any more, do we Henry?"

The Guard Advice suddenly looked over to him, confused and stunned by this unexpected turn of events. "Any more? What does he mean? How does he know you? Wait, what's going on here?"

Henry opened his mouth, but the Marquis allowed himself to speak on his behalf. "Henry indeed knows me, but no more than you know him."

"Just a minute," he said tensely, interrupting him and trying to come to grips with what was happening. "Just how exactly does this man know you, and what is going on here?" He thought this was a meeting between strangers and now it seemed the only one outside of the circle was he; all at once he became excited, demanding answers as well as an explanation for the apparent deceit.

"Calm yourself, Mr. Henderson," the Marquis replied, now mentioning his name, which only further exacerbated the confusion.

"Just a minute, how do you know me and my name? Did he tell you? I demand an explanation!" He stood up, quite anxious, and began to back away from the conspirators.

"Please sit. I assure you everything will be explained."

"I want answers, and I want them now!"

But the Marquis was patient. "Henry arranged this meeting," he replied. "I received his rider a few weeks back and although I was headed to South Anchorage Point I made a detour here."

"South Anchorage Point? That's where Mr. Kepler," he cut himself off. "Why there? What business do you have there?"

"Nothing that matters as much as this meeting now."

"How so?"

"We'll get to that shortly. Now please sit."

"But how did he inform you," he asked, still baffled. After all, Henry had never left the party since rescuing them. How on earth could he have alerted the Marquis?

"As I said, he sent a rider."

"What rider?" But then he remembered. Quickly turning to Henry he could barely restrain his disconcert. "Does he mean that rider you sent to our company? But you gave me your word that my men were informed of our location. Am I to understand you lied?"

Once again Henry opened his mouth to answer, but the Marquis did so for him. "As I said, this meeting was arranged by Henry, and you were brought here on his invitation."

"I'm not asking you, nor does he need an interpreter."

"But I will speak for him, Mr. Henderson," he replied sharply. "The importance of this meeting override any of your distresses, and I mean to waste no more time. Yes, you were deceived, but only in the very best of intentions. Now allow us to continue with the business of this meeting."

A. Ruben

The Guard Advice snickered, astounded by the man's tapered words. "You know, I do recognize you now," he said, his tone piercing. "I saw you at Fort Heritage. You and him," he pointed to Nate. "Now I may not know your business entirely, but here's the thing about Guard Advice. We can either be your best friend or your worst enemy, and frankly you're not doing a great job of making friends with me. So, whatever it is you think this meeting needs to be about I'd advice you to stop for a good long minute, pull your head out of your arse and realize that if you don't start giving me answers then I'm walking out of here."

"That would be ill-advised."

He chuckled at that threat. "I'm a Guard Advice. I didn't earn it by being a pantywaist."

"You misunderstand. I don't mean harm will come to you. I mean it will come to your companion, the lieutenant you're traveling with."

He started to reach over the table to grab him when Nate abruptly intercepted his reach; with all his weight he pushed down on his arm. The Guard Advice looked up, quite shocked at his swiftness, but the manservant just looked back at him with a stern warning and shook his head.

"I'm leaving."

"Stay," Henry said, now speaking.

"And the little sprite finally speaks up. You have nothing to say to me."

"I won't tell you again."

The man looked at him with disbelief. "Is that so? And what exactly will you do to stop me? You can't even pull a damn trigger."

Now it was Henry's turn to chuckle. "You think I can't."

"Oh, I know it. I saw it. You don't have it in you."

"Then walk away and I'll prove you wrong."

"What, you're going to shoot me in the back? Please. At least your foreign friend has the decency to bring along someone with a spine. The only one here that I'd believe is that negro; you know, purple is a good color for cowards and men who'd rather play games than do what is necessary, like kill when they must," he said, directing that last part to Henry. "I'm done here. Thanks for lies, but the lieutenant and I will be taking our leave now."

As he turned Henry grabbed his arm. At once however, the Guard Advice reacted with skill and control, swinging around and throwing him against the wall. "Don't ever, boy. Don't! You won't like it."

But instead of showing fear Henry just laughed, his adventurous spirit suddenly sprang to life. "Ready when you are," he said exuberantly. He couldn't wait, but just then he remembered; as eagerly as he was to begin he was abruptly withdrawn. "Bollocks. We haven't the time now. Care to postpone it? I'm afraid we must regrettably return to the matters at hand."

The Guard Advice took a step back in scare, his jaw gapped as he tried to comprehend his odd disposition. What manner of man was Henry? He had heard that he had barged into the ruffian camp, but until just now he had only speculated that to be an exaggeration; what sort of man sought out danger? "Are you daft?" he asked, bemused. "Surely you're not right in the head?"

"Oh, I am," he replied, calmly shaking his coat. "I just regret I can't accept your challenge. That's all, at least not quite yet. Shall we sit then?"

The Guard Advice was stunned. He just shook his head in bewilderment. Of all those he had ever met on the field none were as foolhardy as Henry; the boy was either a skull short of a brain or just held the wrong way as a baby. Nobody invited pain especially from a Guard Advice; only native braves dared to, but even they learned to show respect. He could easily have broken Henry's arm, pulled out the bone and shoved it up his chin into his skull. Then slapped his lifeless corpse with that limp, putty-like arm.

As Henry took a seat, seemingly unscathed by the episode, the Guard Advice couldn't tell whether he was trying to hide his fear or really was oblivious. "Don't ever test me," he said, also sitting back down, but Henry just turned to him and smiled.

"I'm sorry, but we'll have to do this again later."

"You're out of your mind. Either you think you're better than you actually are or you're just possessed by the Devil."

"No I'm as sane as you want to believe I am, but if it helps you to believe otherwise then feel free. We will do this again. I promise."

"You promise?" he said, almost falling out of his chair. "Do you know to whom you're talking? I could've killed you! You don't stand a chance against me."

But Henry was undaunted. Instead of retreating he advanced, expressing even more disappointment. "Look, I really want to, but you're only enticing me on, so can we please focus. As I said, we can do this later."

The Guard Advice was taken aback, but the patience of the Marquis had reached its threshold and he drew the two back in. "Gentlemen, you may resume your duel later, but time is against us. Shall we continue?"

"Of course," Henry said, apologizing. "And I'm sorry for lying to you," he added to the Guard Advice. "But I did what I had to do."

Mr. Henderson was still trying to figure him out, but it seemed a lost cause, and so he reluctantly obliged and resumed to the conversation. "You mentioned my lieutenant earlier. Why did you say harm would come to him? Do you intend to injury him, or is there some plot you are exposing?"

"We have no intent to cause him injury, but he is in mortal danger."

That seemed fairly obvious. "He's an officer in the colonies. What's not dangerous about that?"

"You misunderstand," the Marquis added. "He is not in any danger from any colonial, at least as long as he remains under my watch. That is why you were invited here tonight, so Henry could introduce you to me. Think of this as a small circle of trust."

"Trust? I don't know you and he lied to me. Why should I trust either of you?"

"Fair enough, but then Henry did save your life more times than you may realize. Did it ever occur to you why he didn't wish to shoot the ruffian leader?"

"Because he doesn't have the stomach for it."

The Marquis smirked. "Hardly. I've known Henry since he was young. Don't mistake a coward for a man who knows his own backyard. When you fired on that ruffian you put the entire party and your lieutenant in mortal danger. Had you any sense of the land you would have realized you were near a rebel encampment. Fortunately for all of us, Henry acted on your behalf. Otherwise, I'm sure he would have engaged the rebels." Henry nodded at that.

"Therefore, and I cannot stress this enough Mr. Henderson, the next time you wish to demonstrate your resolve, don't. I have no doubt of your capabilities and training, but for your lieutenant's sake I suggest toning down your ego." Nate whispered in his ear. "Yes of course, I was just getting to that. Henry would you mind excusing us for a minute. I wish to have a private word with Mr. Henderson."

"Of course, I'll just be outside."

As he left, the Marquis leaned in, directing the Guard Advice to do the same. "Henry doesn't know who your officer is, but I do. I have kept him in the dark, but that doesn't mean I don't trust him."

"Why are you telling me this?"

"Because your lieutenant needs a protector?"

He didn't understand. "You mean a bodyguard? I'm confused. Why? I mean I'll protect him on the field as best as I can, but what is it you're not telling me? Who is Leopaln really?"

He silenced him immediately the second he mentioned his name. "Never speak his name unless I direct it. Now pay very close attention and do exactly as I say. You will go to South Anchorage Point. There your company awaits your arrival. Do not let him out of your sight and whatever you do never speak of this meeting to him."

"You want me to lie to my officer and you're not going to tell me who he is," he challenged.

"Oh, I will tell you," he said confidently, "but I assure you it will change your entire perspective."

He looked at him puzzled. "My perspective?"

"You think this is a war that can be won by bullets and bayonets," he said. "But its not just soldiers that win wars, but leverage too."

"You got me lost. What are you talking about? The lieutenant is not some great general or bargaining chip. He's just a kid who's too young to lead a company, and now he's sick with fever."

"And yet," the Marquis said, leaning back in his chair, delivering the point, "he's leading a company of men, more than enough to protect him, guided by Jhor's most obstinate but experienced Guard Advice; friend to the quartermaster in Clarkstown; assigned to roads where no danger lingers; and whose true identity is known to a foreigner. I dare say hardly a coincidence."

Mr. Henderson sat back, trying to connect the dots, but unable to. Who was Leopaln? The Marquis was right though. All of those things sounded true, except that he didn't know about his friendship with the quartermaster, but nevertheless that was too much to be coincidence.

"I give up," he said dumbfounded. "Who is he?"

"Not who is he, but who is he related to," he corrected him. "Your officer is none other than the son of the First Lord of the Admiralty, Secretary of State of the Southern Department, Lord Archibald Halberd, who is undoubtedly one of if not the most powerful man alive."

"In other words, a politician," he replied, rather oversimplifying it. Clearly he didn't understand the gravity of the situation, but as soon as the Marquis explained that the Secretary of State of the Southern Department was responsible for the geographical homeland of Jhor, the Isle of Maerl (home of the Maerlese), the colonies, and relations with other nationalities the Guard Advice showed a bit more respect. "Alright, so he's an influential man," but all at once then the dots suddenly began to connect. It wasn't so much that Leopaln's father was an ambitious man as much as how that affected his son.

But although his face lit up the Marquis suspected he didn't see the whole picture, and so he explained.

True, the Continental Congress could barter his freedom if they managed to capture him, but then what? How could they voice autonomy as a free nation when their moral pillars were discredited; to barter one man's freedom to gain a nation's was unthinkable for any moral compass. Even the most radical among them would no doubt have to refuse such an opportunity, because revolution by dishonor was not liberty. Any pamphleteer could attest to that.

No, it was not the congress that the Marquis worried about nor the agitators. It was something else, rather someone else, far more sinister, more conniving, unforgiving, ruthless and without compassion, the governor.

"The governor?"

"Yes, J. Lamb McAlester."

He had heard of him, but he didn't know him, at least not in the manner that the Marquis did. "And that it was why Henry diverted your party south after the rescue," he added. It was why he had chosen the town for the meeting and the tavern; he distrusted his surrogate father and the Marquis knew this. He had always known that. He knew Jehannette-Marie and her late sister. How could he not? His late wife and her sister had been the dearest of friends, both taken tragically. And so it was that he and Jehannette-Marie shared something in common.

He knew Henry as a boy, watched him grow up, and when the rider delivered the message it came as no surprise the location Henry had picked. The Ruddy Wheel Mead Hall was a boorish place to meet, save for its uncanny mandate of southern hospitality and Henry's liking to it; as unsavory as its patrons were they were in fact far more civil than they let on.

Moreover, had any of them known about Leopaln they would have sooner protected his secrecy than turned him over to any search party; there were rebels in Lamsburg as well as bounty hunters, and some with more than an ear to the ground, but those in the Muddy Wheel were loyal patrons and most if not all knew Henry; he was a frequent visitor, coming as often as he could, brawling with them, laughing and drinking merrily, and always polite, which was a fact that went a long way.

Thus, it wasn't as much of a secret meeting that he had arranged so much as a meeting in a secure location. Nevertheless, that didn't mean Leopaln's name should be spoken aloud freely. "Now do you understand why he needs a protector?" he asked.

"A bit better now, but why would the governor care about Leo- him?"

"A moment ago I told you this war could be won by leverage, not just bullets and bayonets. He will use him. I know this man quite well. I know what he is capable of."

"How well?"

"I gave him his post, and it is unwise to underestimate him. That is why he needs you."

The Guard Advice shifted uncomfortably in his chair. He was a soldier, not a politician. This was a power play and he felt useless in this arena. "Why me? This isn't my game. Why don't you take care of it?"

"Because I can't protect him every second of the day whereas you can. I will have my eyes and ears open and do what I can, but I need you to protect him… no matter the cost. There is far too much at play here than you realize. I apologize for keeping you in the dark, but for now this is all I can reveal, and remember he is to know nothing about our meeting here."

Chapter 27

The World in a Pocket

Archibald sharpened his collar in the mirror. He wasn't born in the purple, but that didn't flinch his arrogance; much like how his son had been an obligation and not a blessing so his loyalty to the Crown was compulsory; his Majesty had Parliament and he had a son, but if only Leopaln hadn't proven to be such a disappointment. At least Parliament could be tolerated.

But then why were children born if not to serve as an extension of a parent's success? After all, his mother had done that to him, the harridan. He had tried to love her, but she had only exploited his prominence for her own gain, and so he put her away in a nunnery. Such is life. Such is love; if she hadn't agreed he meant to burn her alive at the stake publicly as a heretic or for consorting with evil spirits, or whatever reason he felt was satisfactory. All that mattered was whichever excuse would serve his needs more than   hers.

215

Life was cruel, and only the selfish, capricious, and most arrogant prevailed, disarming the populace with lies and deceit, offering promises but only delivering on just enough to stay in office; and when promises weren't kept the most cleverest simply feigned responsibility, asking for forgiveness, but only doing so after firing enough people underneath. Such was life; such was being a predator. And although his father had tried to instill something good in him, goodness was a moot point in an ocean of predators.

Good people were ignorant and ate porridge for supper whereas he dined on the finest cuts of meat and drank century-aged wine; what his father called pride he called achievement. His father had been successful, prominent in his small locality and network, but Archibald had had a vision of so much more. Filled with a stalwart sense of stature, refinement, and routine he seized upon his destiny with sharpness and ruthless betrayal of any so-called friends that attempted to use him as a stepping stone. In this world, there could only be one great shark and he was it.

He refused to settle for second. He was an alpha male and he knew it. He demanded respect and got it, even from His Majesty. Nobody dared to question him or his authority; he kept his wife in check just as he kept the country and Parliament within an arm's reach. Only his foolhardy son had dared to defy him. Leopaln, the boy's obstinacy was intolerable, but Archibald would teach him: the boy had to learn his place in the world, and if his son thought for one minute that running away to discover his manhood was the way he was sorely mistaken; Archibald owned the world.

He had ensured Leopaln was safeguarded, far away from danger, not to protect him, but deny the boy's spirit of adventure. If Leopaln sought to discover himself without his father's direction he would be sorely disappointed. This world belonged to him, not his son.

Archibald had no intention of sharing power or passing the torch. What for? Nobody measured up to him, neither his son nor any rival. He was the best of the best, champion of the arena. He had the world in his pocket and he intended to keep it that way; Romennal was beaten and the revolting colonies would be treated without pity once Lord Horwick arrived. He was father to the world, imbuing a harsh sense of reality to those that refused to submit to his will. Jhor's navy commanded the seas and its armies were an unbeatable projectile of it. Who dared to defy him? Who!

He had tried to instruct Leopaln early on, giving in to his childlike curiosity about the world, but soon realized that had been a terrible mistake, for as soon as the boy turned eight his expectations were disappointed. The boy just wanted to play with other children instead of growing up. What juvenile wishes! From then on he reviled ever bringing the boy into the world. How could he have born such a disappointment? He scorned his wife, blaming her for being soft, screaming at her whenever she tried to show compassion, cursing her love as the reason for softening his offspring. And so the boy grew up begging for love.

But Archibald had no intent on making the world better for his son, or helping him to fulfill his hopes and dreams. If Leopaln would not submit to being an extension of his will then the boy would learn that those that own the world also own life itself. Just as he embraced all those that submitted to him so he embraced Arrah as his own, intending to cultivate her future to replace the failure of his son.

She would surmount her loss for Leopaln with his grace and magnanimity. He would look out for her welfare, not for her sake, but his; she would magnify his power in ways she could not even begin to comprehend. She would welcome his sympathies, and in return he would make her a woman among women, a tool to bend and a rod to pierce.

Chapter 28

Breaking the Siege

Nate was puzzled. "You lied to him," he said, mystified as to why the Marquis would accuse J. Lamb McAlester of conniving. "You told him that the governor was looking for him, but he isn't. At least that's as much as I understand the matter."

The aristocrat offered him a faint smile; he was pleased to see his manservant using his head. Nate was becoming quite astute. "You are correct, but that doesn't mean the governor will not use him if he learns of him. As you know, he and I have history, but that doesn't mean I trust him as much as I do you. You have been with me through much, Nate, and for that I am forever grateful." He paused. "Lying is a matter of perspective I suppose, and if anyone should understand that I would hope it is you."

As the carriage rode off the Marquis silently glanced out the window, permitting his thoughts to whisk him away. Events were taking an unusual turn, and if he didn't remain on top of them he could easily lose control; such was the fate of negligence. He remembered what had transpired nearly a decade ago as a result of such disregard, nearly bringing Jhor and Bahn into war. Several Negro sailors of Bahn had disembarked in South Anchorage Point, ignoring prudence for a drink and merriment in a local tavern. Instantly, however, they were grabbed and sold at auction despite their protests that they were freemen of a foreign king. Needless to say, Bahn demanded restitution. When Archibald refused Bahn threatened war, and it took Jehannette-Marie to settle it, and both Archibald and the Marquis were impressed if not the kings of both courts.

So perhaps there was another reason for his lying, something he didn't wish to admit but felt in his heart. Love. His late wife had known her late sister, and although both had sadly passed, he felt his heart pull for Jehannette-Marie. He dismissed it though, refusing to betray the memory of his lost wife and daughter, and yet he couldn't shake the feeling. She was an astounding woman, and his passion for her only soared when J. Lamb divorced her, but would that be strange now, to marry her and gain Henry as a son? His heart sank, feeling as though he had somehow already betrayed the memories with that thought; he was perspective in world affairs, but a fool in love.

And how would Jacob receive that? Surely, the governor would resent his mentor marrying his divorced wife; what unspeakable horrors could result from that? He was already unstable. For certain that would unbalance him completely.

At that's when he realized that he had lied to the Guard Advice not with his head, but with his heart. Suddenly, he raised a hand to his forehead as if ill.

"Is everything alright?" Nate asked, worried.

"I just need some air. Tell the driver to pull over."

He didn't wait for Nate to open the door though. As quickly as he could he stepped outside, trying to escape the claustrophobia of his mistake; his mind swirled, his thoughts running rampant. What had he done? He had lied to the soldier, but only succeeded in lying to himself. He loved Jehannette-Marie and now felt weak at his carelessness. He knew better than this, but how could he go back? His head felt dizzy. How had he blundered so badly? Nate cautioned towards him, but the Marquis walked further away, becoming oblivious to his surroundings; he stumbled and Nate rushed over to him, helping him stand up.

All at once he broke down into tears. "I have sinned," he said, condemning his soul to damnation. "Forgive me. Please forgive me." He staggered, but Nate held him strong, refusing to let go. "I have tried to go on living, but I cannot. I just cannot." He took in quick breaths.

"I am just a man, forgive me." He turned to the Heavens and begged them both for mercy. "I love you both so much, and not a day goes by that I wish I had been taken with you. Why has God punished me so? Why? Why have I done to deserve this fate? Why would he take you from me? Why would he do that, for what purpose?" He reached upwards, hoping to be received, but only air touched him. A stream of tears poured down his face before he collapsed. "I miss you both so much."

A few hours later the Marquis awoke. Nate was seated across from him, offering a friendly smile. "Welcome back."

"What happened? I don't remember."

"You paraded in the fields for awhile, making quite a spectacle of yourself and then I carried you back."

"Carried?"

He chuckled lightly. "Yes. I carried you."

He couldn't believe it. "I'm amazed. I didn't think you cared that much," he offered back, quenching his thirst with a drink of water. "Forgive me. I must have retreated too far into my thoughts. Did I say anything?"

"You rambled on a bit, but you did mention them."

He didn't need to specify. The Marquis knew what he meant. "I'm sorry for my display. I was not myself."

Nate nodded, but knew him better. "Perhaps, you were being yourself. If there is one thing in this world we cannot hide from it is the truth of who we are?"

"Very poetic," he said, trying to be evasive.

Nate dropped his face. "I know you miss them, but holding onto them will only hurt you more. You have to let them go."

"No!" he abruptly shouted. "I'm sorry, Nate, but no I cannot do that. I know you loved your sister and probably still do, but I can't let them go. Not yet."

"Then when?"

He rubbed his forehead. "Must we entertain this subject now? I have just awoken."

"From an act you brought upon yourself. You didn't leave the carriage for no reason," he said, forcing the man to face the hard truth. "You called out to them, begging them to take you. I saw you even reach upwards."

"Rubbish," he denied. "I have had enough of this."

"You can send me away if you like, but you can't retreat from the pain. You know I know all about that, and if there is anything I can do to repay you it is this. Let it go. Let them go."

"Damn you Nate I can't!" he said, turning away in exasperation. "Please respect my wishes and find something new to talk about. I am exhausted; do you not realize the toll this takes on me? I am drained."

For a while they rode in silence, but Nate was undeterred. He would not let him carry this burden any longer. At last, he ordered the carriage to pull over. "What are you doing?" the Marquis asked.

"Showing you something."

He stepped out, and extending his hand towards the plantation fields that stretched as far as the horizon. "You carry your loss with you, but everywhere we travel I am only reminded of my loss. You lament on their memory, but I am tormented by what I see. How do you think I feel? I see my kindred enslaved and there is nothing I can do. Nothing!" He became excited. "Do you realize how this pains me? Do you have any idea how I grieve inside? I see my brothers and sisters whipped for wanting liberty, for wanting to live and breath free of the chains that bind them!"

But the Marquis turned back inside, refusing to listen anymore. It hurt too much.

"Look damn you!"

"You forget yourself, Nate. Now back inside!"

"No, not until you see my pain for what it is. I've let it go, but I'll be damned if I forget why I loved her. She was my sister and I couldn't do a damn thing to save her! I watched with my own eyes as she was whipped to death. To death! Do you understand? I know you do! So don't pretend to ignore what I'm feeling, because I have as much reason to hate as you do. I hate them. I hate every last one of them, but what can I do? What can one man do? And yet, I see what you can do and I find myself believing, believing in the impossible! I see a man that climbs mountains while others only talk of doing it. I feel hope with you. Before I met you I thought there was no good in this world, but you have proved me wrong and I am so thankful for that... if she hadn't died I never would have met you. So, yes, I miss her and not a day goes by that I don't grieve, but you are the best thing that has ever happened to me."

The Marquis sat still in silence, ashamed and deeply humbled. Of all the men he had ever met, Nate was extraordinary. He had endured far too much in life, and was a man with nothing left to fear; even Henry, for being abnormally attracted to danger, could still feel fear. Nate however was completely desensitized. He sighed. How selfish had he been when compared to Nate's infernal hatred? He was right. Had he been born into bondage or sold into it he might have felt the same, and although he could never relate, truly, he could hear the torment in his voice, the sorrow and the damnation.

He had loved his wife and daughter and his heart still ached for them, but whatever perdition weighed upon him was nothing to Nate's nightmare, relived every day and made worse by the sight of plantations and auction houses; he had been wrong to judge his anguish as more than what it was. Turning to him and then to the fields behind he accepted his words. He had to let them go. He had to, and unlike Nate, he had the advantage of not being tortured by what he saw day in and day out. "I'm sorry, forgive me," he said, thanking him immeasurably. He took a deep breath. "You're right. I miss them terribly, but fate has smiled upon me in a strange fashion that I now have you as my company, and for that I am eternally grateful. I could have lost them, but never found you. You are a true companion and a dear friend."

Nate happily placed a hand on his shoulder. "I miss her too, and not a day goes by that I don't, but you give me strength."

"Thank you Nate," he said, deeply moved. "And you give me reason to keep on living and doing what needs to be done. And you were right."

"About what?"

"I did lie to that Guard Advice."

"I know, but only with the best of intentions."

He shied away. "Not entirely. I now recall my episode in the field. I am in love Nate. I love her. That is why I lied, because I am in love." He smiled happily.

Chapter 29

The Slave Capital of the World

South Anchorage Point was besieged, and yet its auction houses remained opened for slavery; though bread was in short supply it had slaves aplenty. It lived and breathed the air of bondage, and the business took no recess. It was ground zero to millions of enslaved and its market continued to flourish as long as the need existed; ever since it's founding it had been trading slaves, and in fact its foundation- from the very first brick laid- was done so by whipped human flesh.

It was a city built on the backs of slaves for the profits of slavery. Stacked like cordwood, and allowing almost no room to move or breath, a cargo ship of up to six hundred slaves was traded for gunpowder, brass kettles, copper bars, and alcohol. Then setting sail once again it bartered those goods for slaves, and repeated; its passage across the ocean could cost up to 20% of its cargo, but what was a slave's life worth? A sick one was thrown overboard to prevent spreading and any chained to him or her were simply collateral damage. That was why more was better. It assured profit.

Nearly half of all slaves entering the southern colonies traded in South Anchorage Point, and there was no such thing as a free Negro, as even foreign sailors learned the hard way. It was a city built by one color to serve another. There was no diffusion, no gray between black and white, no extension of rights, justice or humanity, and no apology given for that. By one's skin color was one's fate sealed.

Along the cobblestone streets flesh was auctioned without recognition of the person, as though one were buying hogs. The merchandise was inspected before purchase, and decisions were weighed against what was needed and what would be a worthwhile investment. Teeth good? Whipped or not? Insolent perhaps. Get the little girl or little boy, or the rather light fellow? Pay three hundred for the eight-year old or a thousand for one in his prime at twenty years of age? The younger or older the price was about the same. It was the slave in his twenties that was the most ideal for labor.

Was there a need for a girl in her teens to serve as an all-purpose tool, laundering, cooking, washing dishes, carrying water, knitting, sewing and completing menial tasks such as sweeping, emptying chamber pots or polishing the family silver, or did the home necessitate an older woman- a Number One

Woman as the auctioneers referred to them- who fetched the second highest prices, but who could manage the domestic hands as well as tend to the owning family's children, becoming a mammy to them; valued for her loyalty and counsel she was as religious as she was superstitious.

Families were unsympathetically separated on the block without shame, ripping children away from their parents and taken away in irons by their new owners. Sometimes a mother was bought with her young, but private deals between owners after a sale often short-lived any hope of such unity. After all, once a slave was sold it was considered the personal property of its owner. It was not a he or a she, just a slave.

A few miles away, Mr. Kepler and the company approached the city, minding their step but keenly aware that time was of the essence. If South Anchorage Point fell to the rebels it would open not only access to foreign nations but also could be politically if not economically leveraged to drive support to the cause: the South's economic dependency rested upon the city, and this fact wasn't lost on the besiegers, who permitted slave trade in and out of the city, thus earning favor with both the resident merchants and slave owners.

"All right lads, let's take a rest," he said, bringing the company to a halt. Under the bearing sun, many sought shelter beneath the trees; most were still disheartened by the loss of Mr.

Henderson and the lieutenant and being the only relief to lift the siege wasn't any more reassuring. Despite having searched in vain they finally had had to press on, hoping for the best but expecting the worst.

To make matters worse, the garrison within the city was barely hanging on. The commandant had dispatched a rider for relief early on, and was elated to hear a company from Fort Heritage was already en route, but every day until then was a struggle. By the time Mr. Kepler neared the outskirts with the company, the city was already breached, further restricting communication. Unbeknownst to any on the outside but only the port, the arsenal, and a few blocks remained under the garrison's control. The situation was beyond desperate.

Discussing tactics with his sergeant majors, Mr. Kepler reasoned the best approach was along the seaward side, as close to the water as possible. "That's where I'd make my stand," he said to their concurrence. "All right then, we'll head in tonight under cover of darkness. Move fast, but keep quiet. Understood?" They nodded, dispersing to assemble a reconnaissance party to scout the area; as fighting was street to street the besiegers had largely abandoned any stratagem of starvation or repelling relief, instead focusing on pressing the assault, which meant there was the possibility of fewer patrols on watch, giving the company a distinct advantage.

The Nations: Fraternity

As dusk arrived, the company began its approach, slowly moving in small units, quietly eliminating the few threats along the way to avoid detection. They entered the city limits, moving from one building to the next, keeping watch for snipers and tiptoeing around debris as best as possible. They passed shattered shops, ruined by mortar barrage, but the damage was so minimal that it suggested the besiegers had little artillery. They moved cautiously, crossing a once bustling street, keeping to the shadows hoping not to be betrayed by the moonlight. They passed by a destroyed barricade and several corpses; they winded down alleyways and despite being many in number they managed to stay together, keeping a vanguard in front and a rearguard in back.

All over wreckage accompanied death, and yet in that there was proof of resistance, inspiring the company to hurry. They passed makeshift barricades of broken wagons, smashed windows and looted homes; the brick walls were blackened from fires, and the streets were littered with filth and the remnants of fighting. All over, the dead lay scattered, defiant in their resolve, whether for liberty or the law. Warehouses were empty, eerily silent and unsettling, their wares taken by either privateers or the rebels.

As they picked up the pace the air became heavy from smoke, almost choking, but they pushed through, hearing the sounds of battle nearby. "Faster," Mr. Kepler said in a hushed order. This was it. Despite being so few in number they were ready. With the Guard Advice rallying their spirits they hastened now, steading their hearts and ignoring everything but the clamor of battle ahead.

The noise was getting closer and as they rounded the bend they saw the defenders making a final desperate last stand against a swarm of rebels assailing their position. They were being fired upon from all angles, in front as well as out of windows. Lead poured into flesh as bullet and bayonet pierced and stabbed. The colonials were using anything they had including butcher knives, striking with ironic resolution as they bellowed freedom but safeguarded the Slave Mart.

Passion fueled both sides, and the defenders now resisted their adversaries with unchecked ferocity, disarming them without mercy, for none was being spared to any. Bodies piled on top of one another, drenching the cobblestones in blood; both sides were mad with bloodlust, reacting to instinct and killing without compassion or care to the wounded. Bayonets were thrust into bellies, twisted and pulled out, sometimes dragging entrails along with them. This was survival. Kill or be killed.

But none were more crazed than the Guard Advice of South Anchorage Point. Of the four, one was shot twice but his adrenaline killed twelve before he finally slumped to the ground. The others fought like an army apiece, butchering with precision, never tiring, and despite any wounds were relentless in their genocides; there was no fear in their eyes, just death.

As soon as the company came upon the carnage they burst forward, charging upon the rebels in full surprise, startling them and for the moment repulsing them.

"Thank God," the commandant said, exhausted and bloodied. "I thought you boys would never get here." He gratefully shook Mr. Kepler's hand, welcoming him to Hell.

"How can we help?"

"How many do you have?"

"Just a company?"

That wouldn't be enough. "We have to get out. The city is lost. We can try and hold, but it's only a matter of time. I mean look at what we've been reduced to," he said, pointing to his men. He didn't like the idea of retreat, but what choice did they have? "We need to abandon the city, and I suggest we do so using the port... but to do that we will need a rearguard, and I can't guarantee its safety or survival."

Mr. Kepler paused. He understood, but was there no other way? Surely, there had to be. After all, what the man was asking for was self-sacrifice, for some to die willingly so others could escape. If it had to be done then so be it, but he wanted to consider all options beforehand. "What about attacking?"

"Not a chance. There's too many of them, not to mention we're well below half strength and most of our ammunition is used up."

"What about the arsenal?"

"We still have it, but what good is it if I don't have hands to hold it. We have plenty, but not enough bodies. So, we've been using the ammunition instead."

"All right, what about escaping through the city?"

He shook his head. "We tried that already, but they have snipers everywhere. How many can we afford to lose before running into the main body? On top of the fact that we're simply too exhausted." Although a gentleman, he had drawn his sword and joined the fray, which was a highly unusual act for a commandant. Not even Lord Horwick did that, going so far as to even forbid his senior officers from engagement.

"All right, so we can't attack or go back the way we came without taking serious risk," said the Guard Advice, resigning to the inevitable. "We have no choice then."

"Bloody shame I know," he replied, offering his hand in gratitude. "I don't like it anymore than you do, but we have to. I know this wasn't what you were expecting, but thank you. I know my men are eternally grateful."

But reaching the wharf meant crossing a major boulevard, which now housed rebel snipers, frontiersmen and former rangers of Jhor, who had served their country proudly but were now dedicated to a new cause; for every kill they made they wept a little inside. This was a fight for independence, but it was still blood of their kin that was being shed. As the defenders dashed across they were picked off with accurate precision. A Guard Advice of South Anchorage Point fell, hit in the head. Then another, and finally the third went down. The kills weren't random, but deliberate. The commandant was hit, but only wounded. As he was carried away, Mr. Kepler ordered his men to hurry. Then he was hit.

"I'm alright," he said, checking his arm. It had just grazed him. "Let's go boys. Hurry!"

The company hastened across the boulevard with some giving their lives by aiming for the snipers. The wounded were carried and everyone helped each other, even going back for others; three dropped their guns just to run and pull a dying man to safety, and for that uncanny display of bravery the snipers ceased fire. For a moment the company didn't realize why the shots had stopped, but then they hurried. Had they been able to see the snipers they would have seen colonials raising their hats to them. This was war, but courage like that was still respected.

At the wharf the other defenders joined them, and at once everyone began to prepare. The commandant was attended to, but he denied care until everything was ready. "Don't worry about me until we are ready to go," he said, brushing help away. "What's the point if we can't escape." His wound was bad, and if left untreated would no doubt worsen, but escape was far more important. The plan was simple. Get out of the city, whether by row or by sail, anything that was manageable. Supplies were put on board and one by one small groups made their escape, carrying sometimes as many as eight to a boat; comfort was second to survival.

"All right, you next," said Mr. Kepler, trying to help the commandant to his feet, but the man waved him off. "This is my city and I won't leave it."

"But this is your plan. Isn't this what you wanted?"

"For them, not for me. All of my Guard Advice are dead, as are most of my men. They who remain will understand, or I will order them. Besides, my wound is far worse than I've led on... I'm no good to anyone now, except for something to hold in my hand."

Mr. Kepler nodded, respecting the man's wishes, and solemnly handed him his pistol. "Make every shot count."

"I never asked where you're officer was."

"Dead," he said, gravely. "But I hope not."

Chapter 30

Amidst Southern Hospitality

Leopaln was still weak, but feeling better now as Mr. Henderson helped him up. "Where are we?" he asked, trying to get his bearings.

"Lamsburg."

"I don't remember arriving."

"You've been sick, but I've seen to it that you were looked after."

"Have you been by my side this whole time?"

"I have, yes," he said, lying. "Now up to your feet. We need to be leaving."

"What about Henry? Are we going with him?"

"We are indeed. He has invited us to remain with him, and although I don't entirely like the idea I think we should."

Leopaln smiled a bit. "You don't like anybody."

"Glad to see you're feeling better," he smirked, hoisting him up. "Now here we go."

Leopaln stood up and tried walking. It took a minute, but then once again he felt life return to his legs.

"I think I can on my own now." For a second he stood still. Then he took another step. "I think I've spent enough time inside. Let's get some fresh air." As the two walked out Henry was waiting for them with mounts.

"Glad to see you in better spirits," he said, greeting the lieutenant. As he mounted up, Henry turned towards the Guard Advice and cast a stern look at him as if to warn him against saying anything. "Well, we better be off."

"Where are we headed," Leopaln asked. "I expect South Anchorage Point."

"We could if it wasn't about to surrender."

"My company is headed that way. So, that's where I intend to go; you can either join me or stand aside. I thank you for bringing us this far safely, but I need to get back to them."

Henry shifted in his saddle. "It's about to surrender, what about that don't you understand?"

"Every letter. Those are my men."

The officer was either feeling much better or his arrogance was just a sign of recovery. Either way, Henry refused him. It was suicide, but that's the only reason he would give. "We can head in that direction, but you're men will either be dead or captured. Why get captured yourself?"

"Because they're my men."

At last, and unable to argue the point any more, they rode for the better part of the afternoon until finally pausing to rest. As before, Henry did all the talking to strangers and taking his suggestion again both Leopaln and Mr. Henderson had traded in their coats. "We're making good time, but we should rest," he said, dismounting. The sun was beginning its descent and as Leopaln rested along a fence his mind wandered back to Arrah. He missed her. And what stories he would have for her! He had battled natives, been ambushed, rescued, then got sick and was now deep in enemy territory in disguise. What an adventure!

He walked alone a bit, coming before a house where several children stopped playing. They saw his sword hanging at his side and curiously ran over. The little boys inquired after it while one of the little girls just stared at him in wonderment:

"Are you going to hurt others with that?" she asked. "Mommy says it's not polite to ask such things, but is that true?"

He looked at it and then at her. "If I have to, but I don't want to hurt anyone if I can help it."

"Are the people you're going to hurt bad men?"

"Bad men? Whose bad?" he asked, puzzled.

"The soldiers in red. Aren't they bad?"

He was unsure what to say. After all he was a wolf in sheep's clothing pausing into a mirror of her ingenuous inquisition. How was he supposed to reply? "Not all of them are bad."

"Then why would you hurt the ones that aren't bad?"

"Because," he said, kneeling down to her. "I want you and your friends to be safe. I don't want anyone to hurt you."

"Have you hurt anyone before?"

"I have, yes."

"Do you feel bad about hurting them?"

"Very much so."

"When I'm bad mommy punishes me. I think every mommy should punish her bad children."

"My father scolded me."

"Did you listen?"

"I tried."

"You should," she said, waving her finger at him.

"I suppose so. Perhaps one day I will, but for now I have to help you and your friends. Is that alright?" She nodded and as he walked back he recalled the fight with his father. They had both said many hateful words to each other, but who owed an apology first? He felt like perhaps he did. After all, his father only wanted the best for him, even if he was a bit selfish about it: but for a man such as Archibald apologies were for inferiors-

almost all people were disappointments, from his subordinates to his progeny. To him, apologizing was an act beneath him, subverting his grandiosity and superior vision, and he had no time for such nonsense. He was a visionary leader and he had no need to feel reliant upon other's feelings for approval. He had a big personality, and if others resented that then so be it. That was their problem, not his.

He had his agenda and he wasn't about to negotiate it just so someone could feel better; the world was a dark place and it took dynamic leadership to inspire others, to fire the torch and drag civilization into the light, and if that took threats then so be it. If he threatened to behead someone it was only meant to mobilize that person into action; he was the engine of change, and he would never apologize for that.

He saw the world for what it was, a tortoise needing a push. He advised courses of action to the throne, but only after initiating them already. He belittled other officials of the court, minimizing their efforts as well as condemning them for what he perceived as wasting the king's time; he sneered at Parliament in private, but publicly applauded them, giving voice to their policies only when they served his interests or when his skilled oration inspired followers. He preached risks, but put the blame and failure always on someone else.

He lauded legacy, glory, and empire, speaking ardently on them as well as taking audacious steps to ensure them, including massive transformations of society. He inaugurated higher tariffs winning favor of the business class, but then went a step further and raised taxes, signally to many of his enemies that he had overreached himself, but Archibald was a man of limitless energy, charisma, and exuberance and the public largely consented.

When he spoke before Parliament, isolating the naysayers with thunderous applause, he divided his political adversaries through political networking. He nurtured great schemes that appealed to a broad audience, domestic as well as international, making believers out of skeptics, polarizing those that encircled him from those that resented him. He slept little and conducted business into the late morning hour, pushing his innovative ideas onto others with vibrant passion; he shunned away emotion and any notion of teamwork, dictating his terms instead of listening to others. He refused to tolerate dissent, and became extremely abrasive to those that voiced their opinions loudly in opposition; he rewarded his enthusiasts with lavish gifts and chastised his critics without mercy: they alleged his superego was dooming Jhor and in reply he mocked their hesitancy to push Jhor forward!

The Nations: Fraternity

"I didn't get here by listening to people like you," he often said, demeaning their worth as contributors to society, publicly railing them and their policies as ineffectual and counterintuitive; many resignations resulted. Of all the departments his had the highest rate of turnover, and yet Archibald was immensely popular. The public embraced his vision as did most of Parliament, executing on his ideas the second they exited his mouth.

He meant for Jhor to rule the seas and had no qualm about underscoring that fact, whether in the House of Lords or among foreign dignitaries. Whereas the other great powers of Bahn and Romennal perceived themselves as equal players, Archibald kindly disagreed, asserting instead that the status quo was Jhor first among equals… a remark that more than once threatened war.

"Mr. Ambassador," he once said, belittling the man by not even addressing his name. "Let me stop you right there. First, it is important for you to know your place in this world. You exist entirely out of my good graces, and you would do well to remember that." His smug was as big as his bite. "I find it presumptuous that you would risk the fate of your land and people with such aggressive statements, because I promise you that if you so much as utter another word that I don't like I will return the favor ten-fold. All Jhor seeks in this world is friendship and trade, but you, sir, have approached this desk with coercion," he said, becoming louder.

"You have referenced war, and I will not stand for that! I am as loyal a patriot to my country as any man on this island and you, sir, will have to contend with that if you dare think Jhor will yield to your outrageous demands!"

The diplomat looked surprised. "What are you talking about, my lord? I-I approached this desk out of response. I am here merely to avert disaster, not incite it, but apparently you seem bent on instigating it either way!"

Archibald snickered, as those the man had completely missed the point. "You are responding not to catastrophe, but to an invitation."

"Sir?"

"Never in all history has such an opportunity been laid at your feet, and yet somehow you misperceive it as something lethal. I have no intention of death and desolation. I am a creator, a maker. I wish to invite you to participate in something unprecedented."

"Please forgive my boldness, my lord, but you are speaking in riddles."

Archibald waved his hand in the air as though to reassure him that clarity was forthcoming. "You are in the midst of something extraordinary, and I wish to invite you to embrace peace and prosperity under the guidance of a flagship."

"You mean under Jhor's leadership," he asked incredulously suspicious. "That's of course what you mean?"

"Allow me to finish. I envision a world under a flagship of friendship and unity, bringing together all cultures and peoples into a new world order. Jhor can do this for you, and I am inviting you, sir, to consider this opportunity. We can either weather the storm separately or come together as one, and that is what I am offering to you, leadership."

The man raised an eyebrow. "I daresay I have heard some preposterous notions in my day, but that, my lord, is without a doubt the most preposterous. Forgive my candor, but you have lost your mind! Bahn would never agree to such an outrageous *invitation* as you call it. You are asking us to become your protectorate, and we are vassal to nobody. I cannot speak for Romennal, but I am certain that they will strive to every endeavor to resist your embraces. I believe this meeting is done."

Ever the preacher, never the salesman, Archibald threw into a torrent of evangelicalism, "I have no time to crunch numbers as you do, sir," he said, interrupting the diplomat. "And your words are misplaced. Again, you misperceive my vision of hope for tyranny, but it is prosperity for those born and unborn that I am willing to shoulder the weight of the world. I am offering to lift the burden from you, and carry it. How is this anything but a friendly gesture- to alleviate you and allow you the opportunity to realize your undiscovered potential? Bahn is no doubt filled with talent, and yet it remains dormant. Why? Why suppress such a treasure through stubbornness when another is willing to offer a shoulder? You are on a crutch, sir, and I am your leg to walk. I am not shaming your culture, language or even posterity, for all of which of that is exemplary, but yet it is not realized to its fullest potential.

"Allow me to offer you a shoulder. Allow me to weather the storm instead of you. I am for the big picture, and I see as many new possibilities for you as I do for everyone. What I am offering is unparalleled. We are on the march of something great, something bold and exciting, a marriage of all cultures and people, of all nations. Allow there to be peace in our time. Allow Jhor to be there for you."

The diplomat had had enough, thanked him politely, and excused himself. But he was to find Archibald moved mountains, and as the diplomat would soon discover- as did all those who declined his offer- that his reach was far greater than any had realized: his evangelist followers were infiltrating courts everywhere, from the Old World to the New World, opening talks of alliances as well as inquiring after incentives for subservience.

"The danger of becoming extinct," Archibald said to his assistant, "is that too few recognize the inevitable until it is too late, and even then nothing is done to stop it. It is only delayed, and like the biblical flood, I too will close my doors when the time comes and those that refused will drown."

Back in South Anchorage Point, the company prepared for the inevitable onslaught. Under the leadership of Mr. Kepler, the barricades were strengthened and every last bit of the munitions was readied; arms were loaded and supplies were kept close by. If the rebels wanted the wharf then they would have to pry it away. Almost as soon as they were ready the firing commenced.

"Keep down," he shouted, as snipers began to pick of the defenders. "Find out where they're shooting from and take the shot only if you can." Beside him the commandant was losing blood. He had relinquished command to the Guard Advice knowing time was against him- it was unconventional, but he was dying and so what did he care.

All at once the rebels poured in, firing, screaming, and trying to overcome the barricade with sheer numbers, fighting hand-to-hand, but the defenders held on. Left and right, bodies collapsed, slumped over on the barricades or thrown to the cobblestones; men shouted, bore their teeth and made terrible noise as they drove blade and bullet into the resistors, giving Death a bushel of souls. Everywhere, smoke and fire filled the air and within the iron fury the commandant fell, knifed through the side; as he slumped he grabbed hold of his assailant and buried his pistol into the man's belly, giving to his flag and country his last full measure of devotion. Then he closed his eyes forever.

For another half hour the defenders resisted until at last parley was offered. The garrison would surrender all its arms and be treated as prisoners of war; no retribution would be sought on any. Mr. Kepler looked upon what was left of the company and garrison. They had all fought hard and died with honor, fulfilling their duty, but supplies were running desperately low and it was only a matter of time now; he exchanged looks with their solemn, tired faces and relented.

"You boys did well today," he said, praising them. "Now somebody give me a shirt." He raised it above his head, waving it as he cautiously stood. "On behalf of the garrison of South Anchorage Point and its former commandant, I accept your terms. You have our arms in exchange for mercy and our lives." As they were being escorted away the southern colonials shook Mr. Kepler's hand, as was customary.

Chapter 31

The Machinations of McAlester

As Henry guided Leopaln and Mr. Henderson towards the city, Captain Rogers received news that Lord Horwick was on his way. Romennal had gambled on one last offensive, but it had been brushed aside. With no room at the bargaining table they had no choice but to agree to the terms, including indemnities and colonial islands. Now with the army sailing for the colonies it was only a matter of time before the revolution was crushed and South Anchorage Point was returned to the Crown.

William burst into laughter like a madman, overjoyed by the news. At last, his salvation was at hand. He danced around the room, skipping to his heart's delight, his sanity long since departed. Unable to distinguish night from day anymore, he now wandered the building in the moonlight, screaming for his assistant and damning him when the man didn't reply; his constitution was as lost as his inhibitions, and he sputtered derogatory remarks as often as he vilified fictitious visitors that he reported back to his superiors, who became even more increasingly alarmed by his state.

He laughed when he meant to cry, and smiled when he heard terrible news. He mixed grief with excitement, piercing the air with his volatile affliction, scaring anyone within range; he grabbed his chest and felt the demons trying to push out, but instead of feeling petrified he wept at their failure; he felt fire engulf his innards and laughed at it, embracing it while simultaneously mocking Heaven. He feared the light and kept the drapes closed, sensing a conspiracy afoot by the angels to subvert his satanic embrace.

And upon remembering Leopaln, he collapsed onto the floor and cried for hours. Then dragging himself to his bookshelf and pulling down the tale of Goshen, he reread the stories that his deceased friend loved so much.

He desired naught but submission from His foes, and so He slew them all without waver. Forth and far into the Highlands of Bladaria He slaughtered and the darkness of His shadow cast upon the land, covering it in fear. He pillaged, massacred, and defiled, without heed to the innocent, elderly, gentle or young. He killed all, child or kin.

He forded the great Shan Abhuinn and sacked the thriving town of Shanborg. Then, set it ablaze. Across the lands, His name traveled, and only ash and smoke were left where life had once been. All cowered, even the bravest quailed. The blood ran thick and knew no end, and the lands drenched in wailing tears and the grieving buried their bold; into the wind, the pleas and cries of the suffering were lifted. They begged for mercy. They prayed for a redeemer from this ceaseless plight… and lo, the air answered. A whispering call blew and the last great muster of Highlanders came forth from the uplands.

But He gave no heed and plundered the Danes. His heartless contempt spared none. By His will, all life ceased. Every hamlet, village and town was reduced to rubble, and long the Danes burned, lost but not forgotten. And the Highlanders demanded He reply to their call for battle and so he did, marshaling against them at Shan Kellie, the ancient woods, and there, at the setting of a sapphire sun, He defeated them, laying low their once imposing numbers. And now all trembled, for all hope was truly lost.

William hid from sight, taking to the shadows as a lost soul would, damning both his agony and Heaven for taking Leopaln. He scraped his fingers along the floor, crying long into the night and exhausting himself from want of food or water; death was too good for him, but he would receive its welcome if it so inclined. His state weakened and soon all he could think of was escape. "Spare me not another minute, oh Lord above or below, please, take this soul. Take me now."

When death refused him, he screamed out, bellowing his pain for all to hear. He broke apart anything that wasn't already destroyed and heaved pieces at the wall or into the hallway; he tried to tear the door from its hinges, but failed and so weak he collapsed. As he lay on the floor, staring up at the ceiling he asked again for the light, but only the darkness returned his invitation. He pled for mercy, but the darkness only mocked at him... as he looked into the abyss so it looked back at him.

He closed his eyes and dreamed. Amidst friends, he now also saw Leopaln and happily shook his hand. He hadn't felt happiness in so long and now remembered what it was like to smile, truly smile. He embraced his friend, hugging him and thanking God for their reunion, but when he awoke he cried aloud. He wrapped his arms around his body and held his sides, pouring out his heart until his head pounded and he simply gave up; it could no longer be endured. With what strength he had left he raised himself and opened the drapes. He reviled the outside world, every colonial, and every misfortune that had brought him to this point:

But as he capitulated, his mind reached back to simpler times, to better times and for a quick instant he was awestruck, as though the answer had been right in front of him the whole time. Picking himself up he slowly made it to the front door, boarded a carriage and made for Fort Heritage. Along the way he beheld the wonders of the land, the bountiful life that existed just outside the city limits; a whole assembly of primeval woodlands, birds flying and singing melodies and deer leisurely about. There was a whole world outside his window, but he had closed himself off to it; there were tranquil streams and pebble fords, shaped rocks with overgrown moss and a breeze that softened his pain; the air was fresh and serene.

He beheld the splendor and perfection around him like a blind man miraculously healed. He took it all in, absorbing it. The rays of sunshine hit his face, warming his soul and he felt renewed and once more in harmony with the world. There were no more demons or need to plead; he felt lifted as if guided towards Paradise. As the fort came into view, he half-heartedly expected to meet Leopaln there, but alas his heart sank, discovering instead that Governor McAlester of the middle colonies was assembling a counter-revolutionary force of loyalists. "God save him," he praised.

In New Portsmouth, J. Lamb McAlester retired for the evening confident that his subordinate was taking care of everything. Lawton was attentive to detail and well organized; though cautious he was resolved. With news of the capture of South Anchorage Point he began marshaling a force of six thousand towards Lamsburg; although inexperienced, he was in command and relied heavily upon the advise of others, including those that knew the lay of the land. With the governor's tacit approval, he intended to secure Lamsburg and if necessary engage.

But this was only playing into the governor's hand. He played both sides, and with Lawton in command instead of he supplies continued to the Continental Congress; he was a man of his word... however that was interpreted. He fed the revolutionaries in exchange for terms, which the congress was obliged to accept: while he permitted traversing through his jurisdiction any seizure of property or harassment of the populace was strictly forbidden; of course, terms and definitions were always subject to change when one side was weighted, and as Lamsburg swelled with rebel sympathy he put the congress on notice, insinuating they had violated its end of the deal by "seizing" property; they were inestimably apologetic, but their costs went up anyway.

But it wasn't their worthless currency he wanted or their I.O.U.'s, but instead favors. The articles that bound the revolutionary colonies were weak, unable to tax or draft, and that conflicted with his future designs; he wanted coin and crowd. He wanted an army at his command and a treasury at his disposal; if independence was inevitable he wanted to reign, presiding over the new colonies as its master, or Lord Protector, as he described the post.

But to that end he objected to any notion of states' rights, opposing a confederation of individual legislatures as a dismantling tool to his rule, or inherent liberty, whichever sold to the populace. "One Legislature. One Congress," he argued in his letters; a firebrand for revision, he declared the need for a new constitution. "These Articles upon which the Continental Congress currently operates stymies birth, castrating maturation by inhibiting the ability to tax, regulate commerce, or draft as the needs of war demand. A strong, federal government with these qualities can not only buoy liberty, but also give nourishment to its ripening, especially through sturdy judicial review. What shall we have, liberty or nothing? Only through one legislature, one Congress, can our future and all futures unborn be secured."

He played his cards exceedingly well, grating the congress to the point of bitter resentment, but what could they do? His opinions had following. Newspapers printed his objections, garnishing him immense popularity between both revolutionary as well as loyalist. He took no side, instead drawing attention to the Article's weaknesses, by which the Congress governed and ultimately paid its recruits; the more vocal he denounced their currency and I.O.U.'s the fewer recruits the Continental Army had. This exasperated the Congress, but J. Lamb merely asserted that he was helping them by addressing their flaws. "To reject constructive criticism is to revoke individual liberty of the freedom of speech. Where there is obstinacy there is tyranny."

He then wrote to Parliament, urging them to send aid as soon as possible, informing them of the capture of the South Anchorage Point and how he was now marshaling a defense against the inevitable incursion of rebels; as he stared at the painting of Benito, he smirked. He had learned well from the Marquis, and now his son would learn from him.

Chapter 32

Secrets Unearthed

With news of the fall of South Anchorage Point, Henry urged his guests to turn back to Lamsburg. If they didn't they could be overtaken. "We can't go on any further, not without undo exposure. We will be found out for sure."

"But Sterling Way runs from South Anchorage Point back to Lamsburg and then intersects with the Merchant Road," Mr. Henderson objected. "Surely going back is no different than sitting on the road and waiting. Either way we will be discovered."

"We could take to the countryside," Leopaln suggested, but Henry shook his head. "No, we'd be more exposed that way. Crossing across open fields instead of main roads raises too many questions."

"No more than here," he replied.

Henry rubbed his forehead. There was one other way, a last resort option, but he had

257

been avoiding it; reaching out to his mother's contacts would undoubtedly cause alarm amongst his guests, who might began asking questions into his background, casting doubt on his loyalty. But at this point, capture seemed inevitable. "There is one other way," he said, gingerly offering it up, but then pausing abruptly, rethinking whether to share it or not.

"Well, what is it?" Leopaln asked.

Henry suddenly wished he hadn't said anything at all, but then what was worse, to be captured by the Continental Army or surrender to his mother's southern contacts? They would remember him, but that was all he was sure of; he neither knew their allegiance nor their disposition; hardship and welfare had befallen many, and both went hand-in-hand, especially in war; protecting one's family and assets came before helping strangers, even the son of Jehannette-Marie. So, whether any would help him was perhaps even more of a gamble than sitting on the road, but it was still an option.

"I know some people that might help us."

"Help, how? Who are they?"

"I know them… at least they know my mother."

There was hesitancy in his voice. "Can we trust them?" His ambivalence was not very reassuring.

"I don't know, but we have a better chance with them than sitting here or turning back to Lamsburg."

"And yet, if my company has been captured they are most certainly with the colonial army, which is headed this way, or is there a chance they will be taken somewhere else?"

Henry wasn't sure of that either, but he felt the most certain course of action was pursuing a contact. "I wish I had a better idea, but right now that's all I've got. At least we'll be with someone with resources."

"Resources?" The Guard Advice said, now entering the conversation. "Just exactly who are these contacts?"

"Everything from plantation owners to shipping owners, high society folk."

That was surprising to hear. "And you're her son?" Mr. Henderson said. "Seems like there is something you're not telling us, like who you really are."

"I am the captain of the militia and a teacher."

"And the son of a mother who is well-connected."

He paused. "Yes, and that too."

"Care to elaborate?"

"We don't have time."

"Well I do," he said, unhorsing.

"We don't have time for this. They are coming!"

But Mr. Henderson wasn't going anywhere, not until he got some answers. "I knew from the start that there was something you weren't telling us. So, why did you lie? What is so important that you had to hide it from us?"

Henry rode up to him. "You're calling me a liar? I hid nothing from either of you that wasn't pertinent to the moment. I have kept my word the entire time… if anyone is a liar I suggest you start confessing to your officer."

Leopaln shot him a glance. What did he mean? But the Guard Advice didn't bother turning away. Instead, he walked over to him and grabbed hold of the reins.

"So that's how it's going to be then, huh? Just like that. You're going to undo everything, because you can't man up and explain yourself."

"What is he talking about, Mr. Henderson? What have you kept from me?"

"I have kept nothing from you that you don't already know, sir!"

"Now who's speaking rubbish? Tell him already!"

He pointed his finger at him. "Watch yourself boy. You may not like where this goes. You can try to save yourself, but it won't work."

"Save him from what?" Leopaln pressed. "Tell me! I order you to. What have you kept from me?"

As two winds closed in, one from the north and the other from the south, the Guard Advice yielded to Leopaln, telling him the truth about the secret meeting in Lamsburg, the Marquis, the governor, and how he had been sworn to secrecy to protect Leopaln and his identity. "You've earned my respect, sir. Everything you've done has been in the interest of the men and I respect that."

But Leopaln cut him off with a raised hand, irate beyond belief. He had no words, just anger. How could he? How could his Guard Advice keep something like that from him? But was it his fault, or was it the fact that Leopaln was simply born to his father, a man he reviled as much as he couldn't escape, no matter where he apparently went in the world; he could no more escape his watch than he could escape being his son.

Archibald had brought up the boy, trying to sculpt him as an extension of his own image, but Leopaln wanted to live his own life. He wanted to love Arrah, to marry her and to bear a child with her, but his father would not have it; he never did, not with any of his decisions. He dominated Leopaln as he subjugated Jhor; he denounced individual liberty, applauding communism as long as he dictated.

He was a monster, but no matter what he was he was still his father; a limb could be severed, but he was Archibald's blood, and there was no greater curse. He detested him, his arrogance and his strong-armed subjugation of others; he wished his father would apologize, but that was forlorn. Archibald would never. That was beneath him; even if Leopaln apologized first his father would never reciprocate, or if he did it was hollow. His father was cold and heartless, and of all the wishes in the world Leopaln longed for normalcy, to be average, to be unknown, to become a nobody, ignored by the pages of history.

For a moment he was silent. Then he spoke, shaming them both. "Think about how it feels to be judged by who your father is instead of who you are. I am not my father. I have no intention of becoming him. I am Leopaln. That is who I am." Then he turned his horse away, heading back to Lamsburg.

Henry and Mr. Henderson felt like fools. Of all the secrets kept that was the one that hurt the most; they hurried after him, sincerely apologetic. They had no idea. They had never once considered his sentiment towards his father.

"You're right," said Mr. Henderson, trying to make amends. "I lied to you, and I did it on an assumption. What can I say, I'm an arse. You're not you're father, I know that, but it's taken me until now to realize something about you, sir. You may be your father's son, but you are you, and you're the man I've come to respect, and I mean that. I'm sorry it's taken me this long to say that, or realize that you've been carrying this burden with you, but as far as I'm concerned you're a good man. You've led as well as you can, given the circumstances, and never once have you given up on the lads." He reached his hand out. "I am honored and deeply humbled."

Henry came up alongside, crushingly ashamed. He too hadn't realized the weight on his shoulders. It wasn't that Leopaln was afraid of being exposed. It was that he had to live with the fact that Archibald was his father; suddenly, Henry felt the two shared something in common.

"My mother is Jehannette-Marie," he said softly, disclosing his own secret. It was true to a degree. "And my father is Jacob McAlester."

"The governor?" The Guard Advice said, stunned.

Henry nodded reluctantly. "He divorced my mother and took everything from her, but she is a resourceful woman, and I'm glad to call her my mother." He took a deep breath. "I'm daring like her and she means the world to me. I grew up around these parts and so I trust her contacts more than I do anyone else. If you're father is anything like you say he is then it seems you and I share something in common. And that is the truth, and all of it. Now you know who I am."

"If you trust your mother's contacts then so will I," Leopaln said, accepting his handshake. "We've come this far with you and you've never led us astray. If my men are indeed coming this way then perhaps they can still be saved."

"And what if you're contacts turn us over?" The Guard Advice asked, considering the possibility.

"Southern hospitality, Mr. Henderson," Henry said, believing in it. "Never underestimate it." As they turned back to Lamsburg the winds began to collide.

Chapter 33

The Incident at the Border

Although the nearest contact was nearby, they instead rode back towards Lamsburg where his second choice was. It lay just north of the crossroads, but no sooner had they reached the outskirts than they learned of Lawton's approach.

"Bloody hell! We can't press ahead and we can't go back. We're surrounded!"

"But they don't know we're coming," Mr. Henderson said. "That should give us the advantage."

But Henry shook his head. He knew his men well. "They don't march looking over their shoulder and they certainly won't move on an empty stomach. They'll be scavenging every plantation and home along the way."

"You're father would allow that? That doesn't seem like something a governor would approve of."

He half-heartedly smiled. "I don't approve of him, so what do you think I taught them?"

265

"Terrific."

"So, we can't go any further without being discovered," Leopaln said, "and we can't go south without also being discovered. It seems Lamsburg is our only choice, but if we are to be captured then which side do we pick?"

That was a profoundly good question. Capture was inevitable, but to whom should they surrender? There was a chance that perhaps some Continental Army officers were his mother's contacts, but Henry couldn't be sure. Then again, his militia would recognize him, but what about Leopaln? He would be safe, but not his identity; J. Lamb would no doubt exploit it to some end. But then so would the Continental Congress no doubt; the fact was that neither side could be trusted to safeguard him. Both would exploit him.

But why was he worried about an officer of Jhor? Shouldn't he just worry about himself? He looked at Leopaln. The second he burst into the ruffian camp he had guessed right; the Marquis had alerted him of Leopaln's presence and he had been on the lookout ever since; in a way, the Marquis had placed Leopaln in his trust.

"If we allow ourselves to be captured by my men," Henry said, "I'm afraid they'll learn who you are and turn you over to my father. I won't be able to protect you then. My men have good hearts, but my father has a way of breaking through that. You won't be safe for long."

"So what are you suggesting?"

"Probably the last thing you'd every hear me say."

"No, you're right," said Mr. Henderson agreeing, starting to think like a politician. "As unbelievable as it is he has a better chance with the rebels. He holds more weight with them; they need him more; the last thing they'll ever do is throw him in a dungeon and toss away the key." He turned to him. "Face it, sir. You're far too important. Whether you like it or not you, you're probably the most important piece on this chessboard right now. And based on what I've heard about this governor the last place I want you is with him."

"So, I'm turning myself over to the colonials?"

"It's the best shot we got," Henry said.

"I don't doubt what any of you are saying. It's just I wish it wasn't so."

"But it is, sir. You are your father's son and that won't ever change, but it does give you a hell of a playing hand."

He suddenly realized what he meant. "I could ask for the safety of Mr. Kepler and the men."

"Yes, you could… and obviously ours too," he said with a smile. "Whatever you want. It's yours. You're the piece to this whole thing. Wars aren't just fought with bullets and bayonets, but also with leverage, and you *are* that leverage."

As the Continental Army arrived at Lamsburg, a small party surrendered to them and at once requested to be taken to the commanding officer. Since they asked instead of demanding the sentries, happening to be southern, obliged; courtesy beget hospitality. The army was resting on the outskirts and was well received by the residents, who were walking leisurely in and out of camp.

Towards the rear of the encampment the party was taken into a large tent, where several officers stood overlooking a table discussing plans.

"Pardon me, sir," said the soldier. "They just surrendered to us. We were going to treat them as prisoners of war, but this one asked to see you."

"Southern hospitality," an officer muttered, condemning its liability.

The general thanked him however, and then offered his guests something to drink. "I would ask who you are, but then I already know. I've been expecting you for some time." The party quickly exchanged confused looks. "Oh, yes, lieutenant. I know who you are. I know who your father is, and before you ask, yes your men are with me along with your Guard Advice.

They fought well at South Anchorage Point and I've been looking after them ever since."

Leopaln was taken aback but also overjoyed. How did he know? He was glad to hear Mr. Kepler was well, but if this general knew his identity then who also might know?

"You know who I am sir, but I do not know you."

"I'm General Isaac Hubert," he said, taking a seat. He was tall, his uniform custom-tailored, but there was an uncanny modesty about him. He dressed like one who had been a soldier much of his life, but he was a soldier's general, not an officer's; he shared the burden of his men, holding himself to the highest standard so others could model. This sharply contrasted with Jhor, and perhaps was one more reason why colonials felt so distant from their brethren across the ocean. Whereas someone like Lord Horwick simply expected his soldiers to perform their duties regardless of their condition, underscoring the social stratification, colonial officers, such as General Hubert, viewed their success as a direct result of those who fought and died under their command.

"Permit me to ask, sir," Leopaln said, still puzzled. "But how is it that you came about learning who I am?"

"Because I told him," said a familiar voice. All at once a man in purple stood up. He had been sitting behind the crowd of officers the entire time, waiting for the proper moment to signal his presence. At once, Henry's face lit up with surprise, as did the rest of the party. "Hello Henry, good to see you again. And now gentlemen, with introductions complete, let us proceed forward."

"Are they to be present in our meeting," the general asked, hesitant to the idea. He was cordial, but the fact remained that Leopaln was an enemy combatant; surrendered or not, he could still escape and reveal any stratagem to the enemy. "I welcome an ambassador from Aiegona, but I must protest to their inclusion."

The Marquis smiled. "Of course general. Besides, I expect Leopaln wishes to check on his men anyway. I believe an escort would also be appropriate. Would you not agree?"

"Yes, of course. It would be my pleasure. Any officer who looks after his men has my deepest respects," he said, nodding at Leopaln reverently. But as the party started to leave, the Marquis called out to Henry, bidding him to stay.

"Now then gentlemen, if I may direct your attention to the matter at hand. As I understand the situation there is an army north of Lamsburg, consisting largely of irregulars and militia, but that doesn't mean it should be disregarded. Isn't that right, Henry?" The captain of the militia nodded. He was still recovering from his elation.

"Can we expect a difficult fight?" the general asked.

He nodded again. "Most certainly," he said. "From what I've seen in your camp the best you have are the amateurs I've trained; you may be up against militia, but they're well-trained, highly disciplined, and excellent shots. Don't be mistaken. I trained my men well, very well."

"So what do you suggest?"

"Do you have any rangers?"

"We do."

"Then use them."

"These are the men you trained," the general said, questioning Henry's loyalty. "Why are you helping us?"

"They're good men," he replied solemnly. "Much as I expect you gentlemen are. But they're my men, and I know what you're up against, and frankly you don't stand a chance."

One of the officers took offense to that. "We took South Anchorage Point from regulars. What makes you think your militia is better trained?"

"What, besides my men know the lay of the land, that they can hunt, kill and clean, and survive if need be in the wilderness as well as open you up and fillet you like a fish? I guess just a hunch, but as I just told you I trained them, and if there is anyone more daring than me then please raise your hand.

"I've hunted down mutineers, and you can thank that Guard Advice that was just in here because he killed one of my best trained. I was going to give that man a fair trial, but frankly a bullet was the best thing for him. I know my men and if you're not afraid now you will be soon enough. You think regulars are a threat," he scoffed. "Just wait and see."

Elsewhere, Leopaln and Mr. Henderson reunited with Mr. Kepler and the company. Hands were shaken and stories were shared; everyone was glad to see Leopaln alive and well and proudly saluted him. "I'm very glad to see all of you again, and though I mourn for our fallen, I'm eternally grateful for this moment," he said, receiving their adoration.

Mr. Kepler shook Mr. Henderson's hand, giving him a warm embrace. "I took you for dead, you old fossil."

"Me, never," he laughed. "I'm too much of a stubborn fool, but I will say what an adventure it's been. Not what I expected when we left Fort Heritage. I'll say that."

The company was in good spirits, smiling and happily swapping tales, especially hearing about Leopaln's capture and the ruffians. They couldn't believe he dared the ruffian leader. "It's all true," Mr. Henderson said, corroborating his valor. Everyone was taken aback, having an even greater respect for Leopaln now; they celebrated their reunion long into the night, laughing merrily.

The Nations: Fraternity

At dawn, the army assembled on the outskirts of Lamsburg, facing opposite Lawton's irregulars and militia; both sides deployed parallel to each other, resolved to sweep the other off the field. The revolutionaries proudly held their flag high and at the order to march they closed in with the enemy; rangers moved ahead of the line to skirmish, lying or kneeling; their accuracy as frightening as it was resented.

Lawton had listened to his subordinates and placed the militia on the left while the irregulars were aligned to the right, giving what seemed to be a weighted flank; deception was an art of war, and as the distance closed between the two armies part of the militia poured into Lamsburg, seizing homes and pulling residents out into the streets; the women screamed as their husbands were brutally beaten and their homes set ablaze.

"My God," Henry said aloud, very disappointedly, and grabbing a rifle. He had stayed behind in the camp along with Leopaln, the Guard Advice and the company. "That is not what I trained them to do!" He started running, but Leopaln caught him.

"You can't take them all on by yourself!"

"Sure I can."

"Come on, be realistic," he said.

"Are you offering to help?"

Leopaln shook his head. He wasn't a traitor. "I can't."

273

"Look they're my men. They're my problem. You sit here and don't worry about it. If they so much as point their guns at me then I will put them down, but I'm hoping it won't come to that."

Mr. Henderson spoke up. "That's so, huh. We've had this conversation before remember. And while I believe you're just crazy enough to go in there I seriously doubt you have it in you to pull the trigger."

"This time I will," he said assuredly. "After all, I learned from you."

He smirked, walking over. "We'll see about that."

"And just where do you think you're going," Mr. Kepler wanted to know. "You're not joining him?"

"Well I'm sure not sitting on my arse while that's happening to innocent folk." He approached the sentries guarding them and demanded a rifle. They just laughed. "Is that funny to you," he said pointing to the flames rising high in the sky. "Now give me a damn rifle and make yourself useful. All of you on your feet, now!"

The company obeyed, but exchanged looks of confusion. Were they all about to become traitors? "That is our side," Mr. Kepler said, loudly objecting. "We're not about to engage them!"

"Yes, we are," he replied, turning to his compatriot. His voice was definitive. "Because of all the battles I've ever fought in, especially against Romennal, this is the first time I've ever felt right about what I'm about to do."

Mr. Kepler stepped closer. "If you go then you go alone, but I can't vouch for you if they court martial you, and these boys are staying right where they are. They've fought enough."

"The fight is never over, you know that."

"I know that these boys have seen enough blood to last two lifetimes. This isn't our fight. Let it be."

"But they're killing innocent people!"

"That's what happens in war," he said, vehemently. "People die. We were there in South Anchorage Point. We saw it! Everywhere there were bodies, but we carried on. That's the mission. That's what you focus on! So people die. That's life. It's not our fight. Don't make it yours."

"When did you become so soft?"

"I'm being realistic! You're just as stubborn as ever, but if you want to fight then go, but it's not our fight and I won't stand by your decision. I'm not a traitor and neither are these boys; they're all loyal to their country!"

"As am I! But this can't stand. It's not right!"

"Why? You've seen this before. There's nothing new here, it's just death. Why is this any different? What is so special about these people? What?"

He stared down at the ground. Then he turned to Henry as he answered, explaining why. "Because they looked after the lieutenant. He was sick and Henry brought him here. It was right after our rescue. I protested, thinking we were being led astray, but it turned out that he was only trying to help. These people may have their sympathies, but Henry would not have brought us here if he didn't trust it was a safe place."

Mr. Kepler didn't know that. "Well, that certainly complicates things."

"Does it? Or can we put our skills to good use," he said, begging his compatriot now to join him. "We've seen our fair share and I can't imagine what you and the boys went through in the city, but if ever there was a reason to go against the contrary it is this. But I'll understand if you refuse. I can't ask you, or the boys. I can only tell you why I am."

Mr. Kepler sighed. Of all the battles, of all the wars, from Fort Heritage to here, he felt unsure. It was the first time he had ever questioned his heart, but as he looked over to Leopaln he knew it was the right thing to do. "We looked for you sir, and when we couldn't find you we had to carry on with the mission. Until yesterday, we took you for dead. Now we've learned that not only are you alive, but that this town protected you. So what will it be, sir? What are your orders?"

If there was any liability it was on the ranking officer, and so everyone looked to him. What was his call? Should they take up arms or not; the only person who might face castigation would be Leopaln, but then would Jhor punish him; would his father allow that insult to his reputation? A faint but very satisfied slap-in-the-face smile spread across his face:

"Much has happened since we left Fort Heritage," Leopaln said. "We have shared experiences together and apart, and I hope in the process I have earned your respect as your commanding officer. I would never ask any of you to do something I won't do first." Then he turned to the sentries and bid them to release them. "We're all brethren, but I won't stand for that. Now allow us to save those people." The sentries, having heard the exchange, resigned and lowered their arms.

"Once more unto the breach," Mr. Henderson shouted and the company grabbed arms and rushed forward.

They tore into Lamsburg, firing at the militia and colliding with them, breaking jaws and bayoneting without mercy; no quarter was offered to anyone who was caught. They emptied volley after volley, scattering about or holding together, but slowly pushing the assailants back.

"Traitor!" a militiaman shouted at Henry, who tried to kill him, but Henry fired first. He bolted around corners, taking precise aim at his former unit. One by one he dropped them, until he became their number one priority; they charged after him, firing and welding knives, but his suicidal daring terrified them as he engaged four at once; Mr. Henderson had his back though and Mr. Kepler had his.

They fought building to building, saving the Muddy Reed from the torch, and bellied just as many as they fired at, but on the militia came, resolved and bitter that Henry would dare oppose them. He had been more than their captain. He was their teacher, guiding them just as he did with his own students, issuing practice after practice until perfection. They may have just been militiamen, but they fought just as hard as any well-trained soldier of Jhor, Romennal, or Bahn.

And as Leopaln engaged, he took aim at a mounted officer slashing his saber at residents. It hit him and the man fell, but as Leopaln rushed closer he stopped in his tracks at the rider he had just dismounted. Amidst the fighting he looked in shock at the dying figure of William, who was grasping onto his last few seconds of life. Instantly, Leopaln rushed over and grabbed his friend, clasping him in his arms as he suddenly burst into tears. But William couldn't speak. He could only see Leopaln cradle him, and all at once joy spread across his face. He couldn't believe it. This was the happiest moment of his life. He started to reach up to touch his face, but the end came, and as death seized him he resigned contently:

William had heard about Lawton's assembly upon reaching Fort Heritage and felt a change of scenery would do him some good; though reluctant the commandant there had agreed. And so, William joined up, serving as its quartermaster, and as battle broke he couldn't help but join in the fray…

Chapter 34

The Arrival of Lord Horwick

In the grand ballroom, Arrah entered gracefully, a woman reborn. She captured her audience, who marveled at her beauty. She was a woman refined, no longer middle class, but among aristocrats; gowned by Jehannette-Marie, she sparkled, astounding even His Majesty, who stood in awe of her powerful allure; she instantly stole his heart and he stuttered; diplomats present stood amazed.

Archibald then approached, bowed to His Majesty, and introduced her as his daughter. "If your Majesty wishes."

"His Majesty does," the king said, respectfully bowing to her as he offered her his hand. As the music began, they walked to the center of the room with him unable to take his eyes off of her. She took his breath away and he felt his heart beat faster; he had never felt this way before, and he insisted on a second dance. From afar, Archibald smiled wily.

The Nations: Fraternity

Back in Lamsburg, Lawton's forces were routed and the Continental Army began marching northwards. When J. Lamb condemned its seizure of stores, threatening to cut supplies off altogether the congress responded by ordering General Hubert to take whatever he needed. They had had enough of the governor. Plantations were suddenly robbed, but respectfully; no one was hurt and courtesy was extended.

Journeying along with them was Leopaln, Mr. Henderson, Mr. Kepler and the company, who though still treated as prisoners of war, were thanked for their efforts; the same rangers that had shot at them in South Anchorage Point were now strangely thanking them again. It was a world all unto itself, but southern hospitality was like that. But Leopaln had no reason to be thankful. He just walked in silence, shouldering the guilt. If only he had not fired. If only he had not saved Lamsburg, perhaps then his friend would still be alive. He had held him until the end, forgetting all else around him, and then refusing to let anyone else help him bury him.

"You can't blame yourself," Henry said, trying to help. In the fray, he had looked over to see Leopaln recognize his friend and run over to him. "You did what you thought was right. There was no way you could have known."

But Leopaln said nothing. He just walked ahead, and for weeks said nothing, keeping to himself, and casting a brooding look to any who tried to assure him; it was his fault. There was no escaping that fact; he shouted in his sleep, replaying the shot over and over; nothing his Guard Advice had to say helped, and he drifted further, allowing the abyss to take him; all he could think about was Arrah, and hoped one day to feel her embrace. He missed her so much and cried himself to sleep thinking of her. The more he sank the more he thought of her.

And as the Continental Army camped at the border of the northern colonies, sensing victory at hand, Lord Horwick disembarked.

www.ingramcontent.com/pod-product-compliance
Lightning Source LLC
Chambersburg PA
CBHW060853250626
47159CB00008B/2715